# MERAB'S BEAUTY
## AND OTHER STORIES

# TORGNY LINDGREN

# MERAB'S BEAUTY

## AND OTHER STORIES

*Translated from the Swedish by*
Mary Sandbach

COLLINS HARVILL
8 Grafton Street, London W1
1989

COLLINS HARVILL
William Collins Sons & Co. Ltd
London·Glasgow·Sydney·Auckland
Toronto·Johannesburg

BRITISH LIBRARY CATALOGUING IN PUBLICATION DATA

Lindgren, Torgny
Merab's beauty and other stories.
I. Title   II. Merabs skönhet. *English*
839.7′374 [F]

ISBN 0-00-271510-4

*Merab's Beauty* first published in Sweden
under the title *Merabs skönhet*, 1983.
The last three stories are from
*Legender* first published in Sweden, 1986,
both by P. A. Norstedt & Soners Forlag, Stockholm.

First published in Great Britain in 1989 by Collins Harvill.

*Merab's Beauty* © 1983 by Torgny Lindgren
*Legender* © 1986 by Torgny Lindgren
Translation © 1989 by William Collins Sons & Co. Ltd

Set in Linotron Ehrhardt
by Wyvern Typesetting Limited
Printed and bound in Great Britain by
T. J. Press (Padstow) Ltd, Padstow, Cornwall

# Contents

The Publishers gratefully acknowledge the contribution made by The Swedish Institute towards the cost of this English translation.

MERAB'S BEAUTY
AND OTHER STORIES

# Tailor Molin

Molin had learnt tailoring in Jörn. But what he made was no good.

An overcoat for Nylundius the preacher, the man who pretty certainly was the father of Isabella Stenlund's illegitimate boy; the coat was far too small in the waist and horribly broad across the shoulders. It was impossible to preach in it. And a coat for Sabina of Avabäck, but it was so tight that Sabina couldn't button it up. And the black suit for Konrad Israelsson of Lakaberg: it was so badly cut that he could only wear it in church, for there it couldn't be seen.

After that there was no one who would have anything made by Molin.

The Molins had moved into Sara Lundmark's house, the little house this side of Inreliden after she was dead. It was Jacob Lundmark's Gerda who had charge of the place. She thought it would be a good thing to have someone looking after the house.

"It's pride," said Tailor Molin; "they've always been proud in these parts. And poverty. They haven't the money for tailor-made clothes."

His woman, Judith, was large and handsome, her hair was black and wavy and she looked as if she had painted round her eyes, though in fact she had not; she had dimples and she often laughed to show her splendid teeth. No one could explain how he had got hold of her, how he had conquered her, for he was a poor thing. He had a hump. Not a big hump, but all the same.

And people said: "With his sharp little needle in that seam of hers."

9

But they were childless. And people said: "He sews crookedly and his needle is too weak."

He bought dungaree cloth from Umeå and made overalls, both tops and trousers and he sold them at Lycksele market. And he said: "Folly is exalted while excellent men are degraded."

He had wanted to make tail-coats, morning-coats and frock-coats, not overalls.

But just the same it brought him in a few crowns.

All his life he went on making overalls, and today you can still find overall tops sewn by him.

Even after he did well with his wall-hangings he sewed overalls now and then.

But it was like this with the wall-hangings.

One evening he made a hanging of bits and pieces; there was corduroy, blue serge, dungaree cloth and denim, he made a wall-hanging and also a frame to go round it made of moleskin and he put two chicken rings on it to hang it up by. He sewed his hanging only to gladden his heart and because he had nothing else to do. And in the middle of the hanging it said in blue letters:

REJOICE WITH TREMBLING

Anton Lundmark from Lakaberg came and caught sight of the hanging; he had really come to get a new lining for his dogskin fur coat, he had three homesteads up at Malå which he was obliged to visit in the winter and then he needed a dogskin fur coat. He had two: this was his old one, and then he caught sight of the hanging and so he said: "I can give you two crowns for that hanging."

And that wasn't a bad offer. But Tailor Molin hesitated all the same.

"If you order a suit then you can have the hanging as well," he said.

"I have suits," said Anton Lundmark. "And clothes are only for outward show. But that hanging now, it's about the soul and eternity."

On no account was he going to say that he didn't want a badly made suit, he wanted to be finely, inoffensively and piously dressed. He had his suits made in Norsjö, he could afford it and he was a juryman; the clothes he wore had to display power and dignity.

"I only took those words out of the psalms," said Tailor Molin.

"I know," said Anton Lundmark. "But you have made them great, and sewn them so that they can be hung up on a wall. Words can always be found, but they first come alive when you say them or spell them or hang them up on a wall."

That testimony from Anton Lundmark stuck fast in Tailor Molin's mind. He never forgot it, he knew it word for word as long as he lived; almost everything he heard he was able to repeat word for word as long as he lived, and he lived right up to 1947. During his last years he was blind, then he sewed only with his fingers.

And two crowns was money all the same.

And his wall-hangings were beautified and decked out with symbols and pictures of which Tailor Molin alone knew the meaning.

Later, when Anton Lundmark had gone, Tailor Molin said to Judith: "Words have raised up the man who stumbled and to faltering knees they have given strength. I may as well put together another couple of hangings."

And he sewed two hangings that very evening, HOME SWEET HOME MY SAFETY'S SHIELD and CHARITY NEVER FAILETH.

It was Gerda Lundmark, Jacob's Gerda, and Evald Sundström from Morken who bought these hangings: Evald had a brother to whom he intended to give the hanging, that was the hanging about Charity; they were deadly enemies, those brothers.

And people came to ask if he had not more hangings, and many knew themselves what was to be put on them, and that was words from the Bible and old proverbs and thoughts that had been passed down.

And Tailor Molin accepted the orders and to Judith he said: "Clothes are a worldly matter. But words are the bread of life." However many he made, they were all sold.

And even Konrad came wanting two hangings. On one it said:

KONRAD ISRAELSSON

and on the other:

KONRAD FROM LAKABERG

And one he was going to put up in the kitchen and the other in the parlour.

But after a time, after some months, all the houses round about had wall-hangings, and no more were needed.

Then Judith said: "If you sew them I will sell them."

And that's what they did. Though Tailor Molin said: "But you should not need to."

"You know well enough, Molin," she said, "that I am quite able to walk to the end of the earth."

He sewed, they were the same words he had sewn for the folk in Morken and Inreliden, and Kullmyrliden and Lakaberg and Sikträsk, but he made most of them with MY HOME MY JOY AND HAPPINESS and IN MY DISTRESS I CRIED UNTO THE LORD and Judith rolled them up and put them into the birch-bark basket she carried on her back and went round selling them.

And Tailor Molin's wall-hangings were also a success in Risliden and Björkås and Kallisberg and Bjursele and Nyberg and Avaliden and Manjaur and Rålund, yes even in Norsjö itself.

But in Finnträsk there was a man called Holmberg, Otto Holmberg.

He was a widower and kept the smithy. He was large and fat and had a full beard. He played the accordion. He kept sheep. It was there Judith stayed, there with him.

It was like this.

She knew how to make cheese from sheep's milk, and she

promised to teach him how to do it. He had bought a hanging; he would fetch the rennet she needed from Avaberg. It was the following night before he came back. The rennet had to lie for twelve hours in salt water, so she was obliged to stay until the next day.

Before they went to bed he played the accordion for her.

And when night came he wanted to lie with her, it was in the kitchen. She had made a bed for herself on the kitchen settle.

"Don't violate me," she said. "Don't do anything so mad."

"You are too good for Tailor Molin," he said. "You need a real man. A man like an Ardennes stallion."

"Where should I go with my shame?" she said.

"I haven't got a hump," said Otto Holmberg. "Feel up my back, it's like a byre door."

"Tailor Molin's hump is so small," she said. "I never think about that little hump."

"I've lain alone for three years," he said. "It's like perishing from thirst."

"It is Tuesday today," she said. "Tailor Molin is waiting for me, before the weekend I must be back in Inreliden."

"It's impossible for a man alone to keep himself warm. Solitude is like frost and like frozen ground."

"I won't do it," she said. "I'm not a loose liver; because I go about selling hangings I'm not bad."

But he did not listen to her. "A single log does not burn," he said. He grew wild and furious and his hands were like pincers; she could not defend herself.

And after she had made the sheep's-milk cheese the next morning she stayed there. She could not bring herself to go home to Tailor Molin and say: "Otto Holmberg in Finnträsk has lain with me; he was like a wild animal. I was only going to make sheep's-milk cheese for him. He played the accordion for me. He was like a ravenous wolf. He quite lost his head."

And she said to Otto Holmberg, "Now I am a lost woman."

And so she stayed there. She was there for four years, and people said to her: "But you are married to Tailor Molin."

"Yes," she said. "And I can never give him up."

It was Anton Lundmark who went and told Tailor Molin; he did it out of Christian love. He thought that Tailor Molin had a right to know what most people knew already.

"So she's left you," he said, "and moved in with that Otto Holmberg in Finnträsk."

That was on Saturday. He'd thought she would come home that evening. She'd said: "At the latest on Saturday. When the basket is empty I shall come home. At the latest on Saturday evening."

And afterwards people asked Anton Lundmark: "But what did he say when you told him about it?"

"He said nothing. But he seemed to get the shivers. And he cut his hand with his razor-blade. He was holding his razor-blade to rip up cloth."

"So he was sitting sewing? A wall-hanging?"

"Yes, he had sewn HE REMAINETH DEAD WHO but he had stopped there and I bandaged his hand. 'You mustn't bleed to death for her sake,' I said. 'She's wonderfully handsome, but she is not worth your sacrificing your life.' And I made him a cup of coffee, for he was as it were helpless.

"And I said to him: 'That's the way of adulteresses: they enjoy themselves to the full and then they wipe their mouths.'"

"But he said nothing?"

"No, he was as quiet as a lamb is with the man who shears it, and I had to help him into bed, for he seemed to be paralysed. But it was clean and well made there in his bed, so dirty she isn't; however, even if he now manages, I shall send Eva there with a bit of bread and pickled pork."

But on Monday he sat sewing again. He was finishing that hanging, there was only DOTH NOT LOVE that was missing, and after that he did nothing for two weeks but sew hangings, and when Eva, Anton Lundmark's Eva, came with pickled pork and a bit of bread and a couple of litres of skimmed milk, he had a whole pile of hangings by his feet. And he told her he did not lack for anything, he had bought cheese and hard bread and pork in Kullmyrliden; as yet he was not any sort of pauper, he did not want alms, she could take the food back to Anton. And Eva she did not gainsay him. She'd learnt from Anton Lundmark never to contradict. She was quiet and meek. Anton Lundmark was her head. She was pale and rather thin; she had some sort of heart trouble. But she did not dare to take home those bits of food. Anton Lundmark was an upright man but he hated ingratitude. He loved his neighbour but he wanted him to be respectful, so Eva was obliged to bury the pork and bread in the heap of manure by the summer byre.

After that Tailor Molin went himself to sell his wall-hangings, and people learned how things were: they knew that Judith had deserted him, that she lived with that Otto Holmberg in Finnträsk, so they bought from him, to be some sort of comfort to him in his misery, even those who had already bought hangings, to give him a bit of happiness.

But compassion is not long-lasting, it devours itself, so he was later forced to hit on something else.

That was how it came about that he began to tell his stories, that's the explanation. And his stories, they still exist, they are like his wall-hangings and his overall tops.

First he was given a cup of coffee and a bit of bread, then he reeled off a story; and he chose carefully between them – it would not do to talk about just anything to anyone – and then he could sell a hanging.

And people said: "They are darker than they used to be, those hangings of yours."

"That depends on the cloth," he said.

For the most part they were stories that people had already heard, they always knew the end, but they wanted to hear the words. The words were unusual: the events were not remarkable. And the people he told stories about were all of them old

15

acquaintances. A story is only a picture, said Tailor Molin, and he even told stories about people who were still alive, but that didn't matter for it was the truth – the sum of many words is always in some way the truth.

And they said: "He's like a book of chronicles."

And people who did not want to have a hanging, they didn't offer coffee and they never asked: "How did things go in this place or that and for this man or that woman, you who know everything?"

He knew the words by heart, at least that's what he said – sermons he'd heard, letters that he'd been allowed to read and stories he'd heard from others and those he himself had told sometime in the far past.

If you count the first year when he was brushing up his memory and the last three years when he only went out for two weeks in the year, it added up to thirty-eight years of wall-hangings, story-telling and now and then overalls.

But he never went to Finnträsk, he was afraid of meeting Judith.

Then Eva Lundmark, Anton's Eva, died; it was her heart.

By then Judith had lived in Finnträsk for four years. She was just as handsome as before, and her sheep's-milk cheese was even sold in a shop in Skellefteå.

Then Anton Lundmark went to Finnträsk; he knew that Otto Holmberg had gone to Lycksele to sell sheepskin rugs. It was in March and he had his boat-shaped sledge and on the horse his hoop of bells.

"How long will you live in sin like this?" he said to Judith.

She said nothing. But she set out cheese and coffee; you can put sheep's-milk cheese in coffee and eat it with a spoon.

"He who sins, he is of the devil," said Anton Lundmark.

And what could she say?

"The chaff will be burnt up with unquenchable fire."

Yes, that was how it was.

"Those who live in sin shall pass away to eternal punishment, but the righteous to eternal life."

And she was obliged to hold her tongue and agree: the righteous shall pass on to eternal life.

"And now I need a housekeeper. Someone to look after the house, who can cook. Eva had heart trouble, and was bidden home; she was recalled. It's bland and good this sheep's-milk cheese, and I have a maidservant, so it's to be a housekeeper."

"Yes," said Judith, "that's understood."

"Someone must take pity on you, Judith, and deliver you from sin," said Anton Lundmark.

She filled his cup of coffee.

"Tailor Molin goes round telling his stories," he said. "Stories he knows by heart. And sells wall-hangings."

And then Judith said: "No one has his gifts. He is like a revelation."

And then all was quiet for a while.

She was not forty and Anton was the better part of sixty. Before they left she fed the sheep so that they would be all right for two days, and she took with her a sheepskin rug that Otto Holmberg had promised her. She had the rug over her in the sledge and on top she had her basket. And Anton said: "I shall pay you with money, not with sheepskins."

And the whole way to Lakaberg he whistled. "Whither shall I then flee from the deep mire of sin?"

When they got back Judith said: "You have not understood this. No, Anton Lundmark, you have not understood this."

Even on that first night he was obliged to lie with her. Eva had been weak for a long time and lamentable and useless, and now he was a widower, and in the first place it was his soul that needed comfort – charity never faileth, charity forgiveth all, God looks with pleasure on love and in true love there is no sin.

And when Tailor Molin got to know that now she had moved to Lakaberg, that now she was living with Anton Lundmark and was called his housekeeper this is what he said: "It is twenty kilometres to Finnträsk and only six to Lakaberg, now at least she is on her way home."

But he did not go to Lakaberg, he went far out of his way in order not to come near Lakaberg. AVOID THAT WHICH MAY ANGER YOU.

Otherwise he never mentioned Judith and no one spoke to him about her, her name never needed to cross his lips. And people knew how it was, he had her inside his thoughts, he could not bring himself to speak of her.

All the same he seemed to be managing; in the winter he sewed and in the summer he travelled, and he never needed help, though of course he was as thin as always.

In the spring when Judith had been two years in Lakaberg, Tailor Molin sewed a special wall-hanging for Otto Holmberg in Finnträsk. He had thought about the words for a long time.

And we went for one purpose: he went as far as Finnträsk just because of that hanging.

They recognized one another, so nothing much was said.

When Tailor Molin had sat there for a good while and they had studied each other both long and well, then he said: "I have made a hanging for you, Otto."

Otto Holmberg said nothing.

"This hanging," said Tailor Molin. "Over the years this hanging has become something I have very much at heart."

And that wasn't anything for Otto Holmberg to say anything about.

"Nowadays I only sew the words I have in my heart."

And Otto Holmberg looked at the hanging, it was rolled up and Tailor Molin was sitting twisting it round and round between his hands, it was as if he did not really know whether or not to let Otto Holmberg read the words.

"Sewn words are long-lived," he said. "You can never know if they will ever be lost."

But in the end he unrolled the hanging, and held it out to Otto

Holmberg. He stretched it out in front of himself with straight arms, and the hanging had dark red borders:

HE WHO STEALS A HUMAN BEING SHALL
BE PUNISHED WITH DEATH

And Otto Holmberg looked at the hanging. Then he took two steps, the distance between them was no greater, and he seized hold of the hanging. He took hold of it by the top and wrenched it from Tailor Molin's hands and tore it to pieces as if it had been paper; the cloth rustled and screamed as it was rent between his fingers, and he threw the scraps on to the floor and stamped on them. Not a single letter was left in one piece; his hands were like a shredding machine. And when he had finished with the hanging he set to work on Tailor Molin. It was as if he wanted to treat him in the same way as the hanging. He took hold of his shoulders and wrenched and shook him as if he wanted to tear him in two pieces, and Tailor Molin's head hit the wall behind him, and the corner of the table thrust into his ribs, and his knees were banged on the floor time after time, and it hurt so much that he would have screamed aloud if it had not been that he saw that Otto Holmberg was in pain too; he was in such pain that he was weeping. They knew both of them how horribly hard it was to live without Judith, and Tailor Molin knew that all the same the words he had sewn were the right ones. In the midst of his agony he somehow felt content.

And when Otto Holmberg couldn't manage to tear and pull and shake any more, he picked up Tailor Molin with one hand as if he had been a baby, opened the door and flung him out, and all the time he never said a word; he flung him out in the direction of the yard like a sack of rubbish and slammed the door.

And there Tailor Molin remained lying. He stayed that way until the Erik Larssons came past – they were Otto Holmberg's nearest neighbours. They had a horse and wagon and they understood immediately what had happened, and they took him home and bandaged him up with compresses and put him to bed and gave him a glass of schnapps. He was there for fourteen days.

And Anton Lundmark told Judith: "Tailor Molin has been having a fight with Otto Holmberg in Finnträsk. They nearly killed each other."

"Is he alive?"

"Which of them?"

"Tailor Molin."

"Yes, he's alive. You need not cry over this, Judith. He's as tough as his dungaree cloth, miserable little creature though he is; they are as hard to kill as an ermine."

And then, after fourteen days, he was so far recovered that he could get up, his legs would bear him, and he began to make his way home.

That day, the same day that Tailor Molin left Erik Larsson's and got as far as Evald Holm's in Avaberg, that was half way to Inreliden, on that day there was an auction of Elisin Lillåberg's effects. And Anton Lundmark was there, though not Judith, Tailor Molin's Judith: he, Anton Lundmark, didn't want them to appear together among people, and he purchased two wall-hangings. "They may come to have some value," he said. "They are, after all, a bit like works of art."

And when he came home he put them on the kitchen table.

It was there Judith found them. She had come from the byre and had warmed the milk for the calves; she was in the habit of stopping with the calves for hours.

She saw immediately what it was that lay on the kitchen table, that it was wall-hangings. And she could not control herself. She unrolled them.

LIFE IS PAIN AND PAIN IS ITS OWN FORGIVENESS

and

IT IS GOOD FOR ME TO BE PUNISHED

20

They were not the best wall-hangings he had made, but all the same she remained standing a long time gazing at them as if she had never seen a wall-hanging before, he was after all the only person she knew who sewed wall-hangings, was Tailor Molin.

When evening came she at last had the courage and strength to refuse Anton Lundmark and say that she did not only need to humble herself, that she had atoned for the destruction she had caused, but that it was when she was seeking to make amends for her transgressions that she offended again, time after time, and that now she intended to seek the true atonement and hold to it for ever.

Anton Lundmark believed that she was contrite, so he left her in peace, for contrition – it comes and goes.

The next day, after they had eaten fried porridge and after she had cleared up there in the kitchen, and after she had seen to the calves and washed the separator, she went home to Inreliden. It was a Saturday.

Tailor Molin had just come home, he was sitting inside the door getting back his strength. He appeared to be almost glad when he saw her, he didn't seem taken aback or surprised.

"Is the basket empty now?" he said.

"Yes," she said. "Now the basket is empty."

And she counted out the money he was to have for those wall-hangings she had sold, eighteen crowns.

And then she said: "There are hangings that are almost like revelations. There are hangings one can't harden one's heart against."

But she no longer went out selling. Tailor Molin wanted to do that himself, and there were of course those stories of his; people were accustomed to them – in many places they bought his hangings just for the sake of two stories, it didn't matter that they were old stories, that they soon knew them as well as Tailor Molin himself.

One was about Isabella Stenlund and the preacher.

And there were sermons that he said he knew word for word. And people certified that yes, it was word for word.

And about the Nikanors and their horse, the North Swedish mare who was called Gloria, not to mention Gabriel Israelsson and his cows, the beautiful Merab in particular.

And the letters he knew by heart; he'd been allowed to read them one single time and he knew them by heart.

One was about Jacob Lundmark and the stump-grubber.

And there were stories we have altogether forgotten.

There were many people who went to Judith when they knew that Tailor Molin was away, that he was out with his basket, telling stories, and they tried to tempt Judith with schnapps, and they flattered her; people said she was loose-living, and they offered her money, they were bachelors and old men and widowers and married men who, for all that, were alone. But they got nothing for it, they knew nothing about man's soul, they thought it was like a belch.

### MAN'S SOUL IS LIKE THE BIRD'S NEST
### UP IN THE TREE TOP

And when Tailor Molin told his stories that was how they sounded. Just like this.

# The Biggest Words

The preacher lived there at the Stenlunds'. The preacher always lived at the Stenlunds'; they had a special preacher's bed. The Stenlunds had a daughter called Isabella. Isabella Stenlund.

He always began his sermons by saying that he was an ordinary brother, he was in no way remarkable. "I am only here so that together we may talk of what is beyond and what comes from above," he used to say; but that was before he got properly started on his sermon, before The Word got him in its power. He was from Nylund beyond Malå.

The meeting itself used to be held at the Holmgrens'; the kitchen there was as large as the portal of a barn, there were plenty of chairs and they had an organ.

He was an unusually handsome preacher, big and tall he was and people said he had the strength of a giant, one of the sort that the daughters of men bore God's sons at the time before the Flood in the first book of the Bible when men's wickedness flourished; and he had wavy hair, he was brown eyed, and he made his moustache shiny and black with some sort of cream. Yes, if you have seen Aron Stenlund, the schoolmaster in Risträsk, he who talks so fearfully, the man they are now sending to parliament, then you will know what that preacher looked like, they look like father and son. If only I could remember what he was called, but his name was certainly something beautiful. Preachers usually take new beautiful names.

Isabella Stenlund was no beauty, but she was not particularly ugly either; she had been betrothed to a man from Fåträsk, but it came to nothing, he was drowned timber-floating. She was thin and melancholy. She was thirty-four.

And autumn was far advanced.

When they had been in bed for a long time, there at the Stenlunds', when the old people had already fallen asleep and there was not a light burning in the village; when even Isabella felt that slumber was on the way, she had had to wait for sleep to come, for after all there was a strange man in the house. Then the preacher left the chamber where they had made up a couch for him; he was wearing a long nightshirt of glossy material and he went on tiptoe and walked right through the kitchen to the little chamber where Isabella lay. He shut the door behind him and sat down on the edge of her bed. And she was frightened.

"Don't be frightened," he said.

"I'm not frightened," she said.

"I only need someone to talk to," he said.

"I'm no young girl," said Isabella. "I shall never be frightened again."

"Are you a believer?" he said.

"I believe in God," she said. "But give myself to Him I cannot."

"No?"

"He drowned Hemming, my betrothed, out in the Vorm rapids. And my youth and happiness He has also taken from me."

"Though His mercy is everlasting," he then said.

But she did not answer.

"I can't sleep," continued the preacher. "It is as if my heavenly father begrudged me sleep."

"If the body is allowed to work itself tired, sleep comes of itself," said Isabella.

"My body wants to sleep sure enough. But the spirit will not allow it."

"The spirit," said Isabella.

"The spirit is like fermenting dough, he presses on me from all sides. He gives me no peace."

"How do you know that it is the spirit?" she said.

"He talks within me," said the preacher. "I hear him. His voice is tremendous and loud."

He was looking almost miserable, as if he was really being tormented. He screwed up his eyes as if to save her from seeing the suffering in his face. And Isabella laid her hand on his knee; she did not want him to feel quite forsaken.

"It is as if the words were too big," he said. "As if there wasn't really room for them in me."

"What sort of words are they?" she said. And her voice was tender, as if it was a little baby or a decrepit person or a sucking-calf she was talking to.

"They are God's words," he said. "Words away beyond the law, the prophets and the Gospel. And Paul. And the Book of Revelations. And the Catechism."

"Do they really make a noise inside you?" she said.

"Yes," he said. "They thunder and carry on inside me like the gases of digestion. And it's worst at night."

Then she moved an inch nearer to him as if she thought she would be able to hear the words rumbling through his flesh, through the thickness of his flesh.

"Like when one has eaten pea-soup," she said.

"Yes," he said.

"Or like an organ," she said.

"Yes, even like an organ."

"Like having an organ inside you!"

"The words carry no fetters," he said. "The words have the force of a gale."

"Yes," she said, "I've sometimes thought about that. That words can be as it were wild and ungovernable. So you have to be particular and watchful about them. Those words."

"The biggest words are the worst," he said. "Corruption. And

25

Eternity. And Wild Beast. And Mercy. And Sanctification. And Regeneration. And Beatification. And Redemption. And Original Sin."

"Yes," she said. "Those words are tremendous."

"Not to mention Love," he said.

"Yes," she said. "Love."

And now he crept up into her bed, she let him do it, it was not only the words, he was cold too.

And just as he was creeping up to her, he named two words from the Letter to the Corinthians: Cold and Nakedness.

And he went on counting up words for her, all the big words that were always passing with the thunder of a storm inside his chest, his head and the whole of his gigantic man's body.

The words lay like a weight upon her. For him they were inside, but she experienced them externally like a burden on her breast; it was as if they wanted to force their way into her, to take possession of her, and she was obliged to get out of bed and stretch and draw a deep breath several times, and shake her arms and hands and shoulders like she did in the mornings to get rid of her sleepiness and dreams. Some nights she dreamed horribly; she did not know whether she was equal to such tremendous words, whether there was room in her for them, but later she crept into bed again.

And he waited for her, he'd seen into her and understood that she was fighting a battle, and he still had a great many words left, and a number of those words were only sounds and not letters and syllables, they were also painful, perhaps they were the most painful for one never knew for certain what they meant; and she stroked his wavy hair and said "poor thing, poor thing" as she was in the habit of saying to the animals to be slaughtered.

"The Spirit and the words and the language won't leave me in peace until I'm in my grave," he said. "If then."

"The Spirit and the words and the language have no end, they last for ever."

And it even happened that he wept. And she comforted him right until the morning.

When later on they ate barley porridge before the eleven o'clock meeting, they sat round the gate-legged table in the Stenlunds' kitchen, then Isabella told her parents that she had given herself to God during the night, the words had prevailed with her. The words that bear fruit.

And the old people seemed pleased.

And then he preached as if inspired and released; he who has beheld the company of the free he is happy in his work, this was in the Holmgrens' large kitchen. "In the beginning was the Word, and the Word was with God. All things were made by Him and without Him was not anything made that was made. In Him was life; and the life was the light of men. And the Word was made flesh."

That is how it was for him: his words were the Word and his flesh, that was the Flesh.

How things turned out for him afterwards I don't know. Preachers, they come and go, they have no permanence, they are as fleeting and capricious as the birds of the air and the fish in the sea, but Isabella got a boy in the spring, she did and that was the fellow Aron Stenlund, he is a miserable chatterbox, he is as it were stuffed full of words, but he is a scholar, and now they are going to send him to Stockholm. And she'll soon be the only one left of the congregation, will Isabella Stenlund; they are dying off little by little.

The Holmgrens who had an organ, they have gone too.

# Two Sermons

# The Word

"The sower soweth the Word.

"Whoso despiseth the Word shall be destroyed.

"There is that speaketh rashly like the piercings of a sword.

"But the tongue of the wise is healthy."

It is also written: "He sendeth His Word and healeth them."

At Storholmsträsk there lived a man called Samuel Burvall. He died some years ago at the sanatorium; it was a haemorrhage of the lungs.

It happened like this in his case.

The Burvalls of Storholmsträsk had a habit of dying of consumption. Four of his paternal aunts and three of his paternal uncles died when he was a child, also his father's father, and two siblings, the only ones he had, and three cousins.

He worried a lot about this.

People constantly talked about the way consumption travelled across the earth, making its way from person to person. Was it by the fogs of winter, or by cows' milk, or was it in the water, or in the sheepskin coverings that folk lay under, or in their breath, or was it in the knives and forks and spoons that had not been properly washed, and each and everyone had their own view. Some were afraid of the fog, others of cows' milk. Some were afraid of the sheepskin rugs, and some of breath, and these bent backwards when they talked to anyone, and many people shunned knives and forks and spoons.

But when Samuel Burvall was fourteen he believed he knew the truth of it: that it was the word itself that was the source of the infection, the word consumption, and he made up his mind that he would never let that word into his body, he would shut his ears to the sound and letters of it, he would keep his hearing and his senses clean of consumption, just as other people strove for cleanliness in the matter of fleece rugs, and cutlery, and water, and cows' milk, and breath.

Thus when he was with people he sat on tenterhooks, he sat with the palms of his hands against his cheekbones, it looked as if he was in the habit of supporting his head a little, as if it was extremely heavy, and the minute he realized that anyone was about to utter that horrible, contagious word, he quickly stuck his fingers into his ears, so that not a word could get in. That which leaves the mouth comes from the heart, and that is what contaminates people.

It wasn't easy, people were always talking about consumption, there wasn't much else to talk about. Consumption was as it were the greatest mystery in the matter of life and death, consumption was like the seven stars in the angel's hand. Therefore watchful and careful and almost unsociable was what Samuel Burvall had to be.

But he was strong and healthy, and when he was nineteen and had to enlist, he had never had the least hint of any trouble. He was felling trees at that time in Vackerliden, and he took his skis and went to Norsjö, and the doctor who examined him said he was like one of David's heroes, he was two ells and an inch round the chest, he was Elisha, and he weighed ninety-five kilos, all of them only flesh and muscle.

But the thing happened that should never have happened.

It was one of the recruiting gentlemen, he had so many shiny buttons and stars you couldn't count them, he looked up from the papers he had before him, and looked at Samuel Burvall, and said: "Well, well, Burvall", to him. And Samuel had no time to defend himself, he was caught quite off his guard, and the recruiting gentleman had a voice he wouldn't anyhow have been able to stop, a voice that would have gone straight through Samuel's hands, and he shouted:

"Have you had consumption, Burvall?"

And he felt that the word had hit him like a bullet, it was as if it had torn a hole in his ear. And he felt the poison from the word spreading through his body and blood. Now it's all over with me, he thought, and he answered the recruiting gentleman thus:

"No, I've not had consumption. Not so far."

And so he was called up; they wanted to make a non-commissioned officer of him. That was in the 20th Infantry in Umeå. But only a few weeks passed after which he fell ill. There was fluid in his pleural cavity and patches on both lungs, and they had to send him back to Storholmsträsk.

And the old Burvalls fitted him out for the sanatorium, they weren't badly off. There were suits and nightshirts, and a new Bible, and white shirts and ties and cuff-links; they knew what was wanted. And Sofia Lundström from Åmträsk came over to say goodbye. They had been confirmed together, she and Samuel, and there was a sort of understanding between them, so the old Burvalls left them alone, for they also knew from experience what it was like to say goodbye.

He was away for two years.

And when he came home again he was cured. His skin was white and he talked Swedish for the first few days, and a lot of his flesh had fallen away, but he was cured. And the old Burvalls said: "If only he goes back to work."

But he said: "Why should I go back to work? Life is better than work. To work isn't the same thing as to survive."

And the old Burvalls had never heard anything like that before. To live was to get a grip on things, wasn't it, not to spare yourself? But he was the last child they had. Gaffer Burvall himself had had shingles, he had a bad heart and probably hadn't long to live.

Yes, I know that you have all heard much talk about Samuel Burvall, that you already know how things were. But I shall lift him up and bring him forward, and shine a light on him so that the very meaning itself may be revealed. I shall make a sermon out of him.

33

And Samuel said to the old man:

"This shall never happen again. That word that pushed its way into me and infected me, that shall never henceforth come near my ears, I shall be on my guard so that it may never again take possession of me."

"But how will you do that?" said the old people. "It is one of the commonest words, that word, people say it every day, many can talk of nothing else."

And old Burvall remembered the Epistle to the Romans: "And thinkest thou this, O man . . . that thou shall escape the judgement of God?"

But Samuel Burvall, he did everything in the way he had thought of, everything that he had worked out while he was at the sanatorium. He got timber from Gumboda, and nails and a long iron tube from Norsjö, and a window with two frames joined together from Lycksele; and he did all the building work himself so that it should be as he wanted it. He was very particular and he was not without skill, and what the old man said couldn't be helped.

And Sofia Lundström came. They had exchanged letters while he was at the sanatorium, and she said to him: "You'll soon be a whole man again, Samuel, you'll be like Goliath, you'll soon take over the farm and be your own master."

And he understood immediately what she meant.

"Why are you setting a trap for my life?" he said. "Strength, and the farm, and being one's own master are trifles, a puff of wind compared with having life itself."

"We must weave life to the end," she said. "We must not let the loom stand idle. It has been said: 'We must both die and live with each other.'"

"But one must never die unnecessarily," he said. "I was near to death, Sofia. To die is to be like water."

"But you're well now," she said. "You no longer have that illness, that suffering, that weakness."

She saw how terrified he became when she said this, and how

he screwed up his eyes, and how his lips began to tremble. He was afraid that she might thoughtlessly and as it were in haste speak that word, and when she observed this she felt that she could almost have burst into tears.

"I shall never say anything you can't endure to hear," she said. "Not a single word."

"It isn't that I'm fragile or over sensitive," he said. "But I can't resist infection."

"No," she said. "If only you could resist infection."

"That's right," he said. "Then I should have taken over the farm. Then I should have wanted to have you, Sofia." And then he continued: "Though we can always talk to each other. I should like us always to be able to talk to each other."

And he moved into the little room he had built, and he had insulated the walls and put in a double window, and he had a hatch in the wall over the top of the ladder where he received the food they prepared for him, and which the maid carried up to him. She was called Eline and came from Kvaviströsk. And there through that same hatch he put out the slop-pail that had to be emptied evening and morning. He was particular about the time, he lived like a clock.

And he pushed the iron tube, a one-inch tube it was, he had pushed it with its head by his bed down into the kitchen so that the orifice was by the cowl over the hearth, and if you sat on the wood-box you could talk right into the tube. I myself was allowed to try to talk to him once, I was preaching in Lillholmsträsk, and it wasn't far away. And I said to him: "Samuel, Samuel. 'Mercy unto you and grace and peace and love be multiplied,'" it was the Epistle of Jude, but he didn't hear me, he never answered, perhaps he had a cork in the upper end. Through that tube he talked to Hanna, his mother, Hanna Burvall, and to Sofia, but never to a stranger.

People have often asked what in fact he did there, what he got up to in that little room in the attic, how things were for him? And I answer:

"He lived."

"He lived in safety."

"He was preserved."


After two years had passed old Burvall died, and Hanna told Samuel through that iron tube: "Papa died last night."

"Yes," he said, "I saw it by his looks – that he wouldn't last long."

"It's more than two years since you saw him," Hanna told him.

"What are two years?" he said. "Two years are like a breath of wind."

"He rebuilt the wall of the stove in the cowshed," said Hanna.

"He got ready the wood for winter.

"He marked out the new pasture by Elof's field.

"He delivered Pärla when she was about to die giving birth to a calf.

"He built new steps down to the cellar.

"And he went to Lycksele to exchange the horse.

"And he made a new beam for the loom.

"And he kept the ice from the cellar.

"That's what he did these last two years," said Hanna.

"Well," said Samuel. "What ought he to have done? And after all he had a weak heart."

"We are going to bury him on Sunday."

"It's all the same to me," said Samuel. "People talk so unluckily at funerals."

And so.

After that life was pretty hard for Hanna Burvall on her own with only the maid to help her, and Samuel up in the attic. But he comforted her: "I'm here up in my room. If you can't sleep at night, or if you have a pain anywhere, or if you want someone to talk to, you'll know that I'm here."

"Yes," she said. "I'll always know where to find you."

People asked Eline, the maid: "What does he look like, does he cut his hair and his beard?" And she told them the truth of it. "I don't know. I empty his slop-pail, and I give him his food. He eats well, and his stomach works as it should, but I never see him, no one has seen him since he locked the door. It's a lock with two keyholes."

That's how things really were. For all those years there was no one who saw Samuel Burvall.

And on Sundays Sofia Lundström sat on the wood-box by the cowl over the hearth in the Burvalls' kitchen and talked to him between twelve o'clock coffee and dinner-time. And she told him about all that she had been doing and everything she had heard people talking about, but the name of that illness she never uttered. It was as if consumption did not exist, as if that suffering was at an end for ever, though during those years three of the Lundgrens of Avabäck died of it, and one Stenlund of Lakaträsk, and three of Samuel's own cousins, and they could sit in silence for long periods. All the same they seemed to belong to each other. That iron tube was like a link or a bond between them, and she never had another man. People knew that she was Samuel Burvall's Sofia. They were almost like man and wife.

And that was probably the cause of his misfortune.

As it says in Ecclesiastes: "Two are better than one; because they have a good reward for their labours."

And as the prophet Amos says: "Can two walk together except they be agreed?"

He asked her about many things and of course she sometimes thought he asked peculiar questions. But she was patient, and she never said to him: "You could very well come out and see for yourself." She answered as if he was really blind, or lay paralysed in his bed.

"If you stand on the bridge can you see Ormberg?

37

"How many panes of glass are there in the gable of the cowshed?

"Are there two or are there three chimneys on Elof Lindström's house?

"If it blows from the east does the weathervane on the bakehouse roof move?

"Is the tree that stands this side of the forest a birch, or is it a big sallow?

"When the aspens shed their leaves as now are they yellow, or are they red?"

"They are red."

And when they killed an animal at the Lundströms' in Åmträsk she usually took with her a piece of roast meat; he was very fond of roast meat.

And she read sermons for him, and sometimes, if he felt he had time, also from the Book of Homilies, that is to say from Luther's homilies.

And he told her whether he had slept well or badly, what he'd been thinking about during the last few days; the birds he'd seen through the window, also the weather he'd noticed, indeed everything that had happened since they last talked to each other, yes everything.

"What an awful lot the swallows are flying."

But there was something wrong with Sofia.

After five years had passed it happened that on one Sunday she did not come.

"Man that is born of woman is of few days and is full of trouble." He does not know what will come to pass, and who can tell him what will come to pass? No man has mastery over the wind to check it.

"I wonder whether Sofia won't make her way here today?" Samuel said to Hanna through the tube. "It's Sunday isn't it?"

"She's probably sitting at her loom," said Hanna. "Or she may be at the slaughtering at Lakaberg. And she always knows where she can find you."

"But she said nothing about anything special last Sunday," he said.

"Or perhaps she has moved," said Hanna. "She is quite free. To Lycksele or Umeå."

"She would never leave me. Not Sofia."

"You're silly," she told him. "You're silly in the way small children are."

"It's true, there's much I don't know. But that I do know. I know it for certain."

And Sofia had a sort of feeling of unease inside her. On some Sundays she only wanted to laugh and make fun of him. She was the way she had been at the time they went to confirmation classes with the parson. On other Sundays she was mostly silent, said nothing about the towels she was weaving, or about a cow that had calved, or about betrothals or marriages that she'd seen about in the papers, or of the children who were always being born both here and there. And her voice was so weak that he had to shout Sofia, Sofia, time after time.

And he never dared to ask: "Why do you sound so gloomy, Sofia?"

And she had developed that cough.

It was that dry, hacking cough, and you could hear that she was holding her hand in front of her mouth, and that she was breathing short, careful breaths, so that the cough shouldn't get the better of her completely, and that she was sucking peppermint sweets so that he should smell the odour through the tube, but he never dared to ask: "Have you got a cough, Sofia?"

And Hanna warned him. "I believe that Sofia isn't very strong, Samuel."

But Samuel said: "If she will only eat properly. Barley meal porridge. And meat."

And people told her: "You should try to do something about your cough, Sofia. You should go to the doctor."

But she wouldn't hear of it.

"When I'm alone I never cough," she said. "But when I'm with people I cough."

Thus said the Moabitess Ruth: "Entreat me not to leave thee, or to return from following thee: for whither thou goest I will go; and where thou lodgest I will lodge: thy people shall be my people, and thy God my God.

"Where thou diest I will die, and there will I be buried: The Lord do so unto me, and more so if aught but death do part thee and me."

And at last the Lundströms of Åmträsk had to get themselves a maid, though they couldn't really afford one, they had so little forest, and only four cows, but all the same Sofia had grown too weak. She had to rest in the middle of the day. "I'll just get up my strength for a bit," she said; and she had red patches on her cheeks, and her handkerchief had what looked like spots of rust on it, and she never went to the sewing bees any more.

And the sort of weakness she had was perfectly clear, the affliction that had befallen her, what she was suffering from.

Though on most Sundays she got herself to Storholmsträsk. Old Lundström used to drive her there, he said: "I'm sure I'll get a cup of coffee from Hanna Burvall. She may be glad to spend some time chatting. She is as it were alone.

"So we've both got an errand there you and I, Sofia."

The last time, in May that was, and there was hardly any snow left, and old Lundström had wrapped her in sheepskin rugs, and he had to carry her, she had no strength left in her legs. That was the spring she turned thirty-two. Samuel had then been living up in his rooms for seven years. And old Lundström carried her in and sat her on the wood-box, and drew aside the sheepskin rugs.

And Samuel was so uneasy and fearful that he could hardly manage to sit still beside the iron tube. His teeth were chattering and his whole body was shaking. He could hear by her voice that she was quite done in, and he realized that she had to summon up all the strength she had left in order to sit there and talk to him. She hadn't breath for the words she wanted to utter. "She's near death," he thought. "She's going to give me up."

And he said: "Have you sheared the sheep yet, Sofia?"

"Yes, of course we've sheared the sheep."

"And you've baked the flat loaves?"

"Yes, both the flat loaves and the thin bread."

"And the scrubbing? The big house?"

"Yes, we're doing it. We'll soon be scrubbed up ready for the summer."

"And the slaughtering? The spring slaughtering?"

"Yes, we've killed the pig, and two yearling lambs."

"You mustn't overwork, Sofia."

"Don't fret, Samuel. We have a maid now. Fretting isn't good for you, it can become a sort of illness."

"And the old people?"

"They sent you a bit of meat. Dried lamb's meat."

After that she was two weeks in bed at Åmträsk, and finally the old Lundströms sent for the doctor. He gave her opium tablets and said she was going through a crisis, but that it was too late, and that it was a disgrace that they hadn't sent for help earlier.

"What is the good of science if people continue to rely on their own doubtful abilities?"

But the truth was that it had been too late for two years, yes for the whole time. And who can know for certain that she wanted to live?

When Hanna, Hanna Burvall, heard that she was dead – it was old Lundström who came there to tell her – then she thought: "Anyway it's unavoidable, someone must tell him, and now I'm the only person left in the world who can talk to him." And she went to the wood-box and sat on it, and she sat there for a good long time holding on to the mantelpiece of the stove, and she said to the maid Eline: "You can go out and see if the calves are in the enclosure." And she was so full of dread that her face seemed paralyzed, and what her lips desired gave her no relief. And she bent forward and put her mouth to the tube and called: "Samuel, Samuel."

And he answered: "Yes, here I am."

And then she told him. "Sofia has died. She died last night."

He said nothing. There was complete silence in the tube, you couldn't even hear him breathing. And so she said again: "Sofia died last night."

Of course he heard what she said, but to hear is not to understand, it took time for the words to eat their way into him, it was as it is when a fever pierces through a human being. He thought: "I'm losing my reason." And inside him it was as black as night, and he took hold of the iron tube to save himself from collapsing, and he thought: "I've talked to her haven't I! I've talked to her every Sunday. I talked to her only a few weeks ago. Death can't come suddenly like that. She was scrubbing up for the summer wasn't she?"

Though after a time he saw that it was true all the same. Why should Hanna think up a thing like that? And Sofia had been ill for a long time, there was that hacking cough and her breathlessness, and he remembered that he had thought that she was going to abandon him, he'd half thought so, but had not dared to ask her, hadn't wanted to risk his life by asking her, if only he'd at least asked her, and then he thought: "It doesn't matter any more. Now everything is over. Why should I be bound to life like a foetus in the womb? Now there is no longer a word that I fear."

And he put his mouth to the iron tube and shouted in despair, shouted so that it thundered through Hanna's kitchen:

"Was it consumption? Was it consumption that took Sofia?"

And Hanna said: "Yes, it was consumption."

Eline had now come back, and after a while they heard that he was unlocking the door, using both the keys, and they heard him come down the stairs. He moved like one who is slow and stiff, it sounded like old Burvall in his last years, and then he came down to them. He had stuffed his long beard into his trouser waistband, and his hair hung down over his shoulders. He stepped into the kitchen and Hanna scanned his face, saw how he had aged, how he was suffering. And she thought: He won't fight against it any more, his eyes are quite blank, he's in despair; he's at once doomed and set free.

And she said to him: "Consumption is only an illness, Samuel. Some die of it, others don't. But all the same it's only an illness."

It's true.

And thus saith King Solomon:

"A man's belly shall be satisfied with the fruit of his mouth, and with the increase of his lips shall he be filled.

"Death and life are in the power of the tongue . . ."

# Mercy

I remember a soul that I saved.

He was called Lundgren and was a native of Granträskliden.

Through the word cometh mercy unto us.

It was after a meeting in Lakaberg, there in the Holmgrens' kitchen. He had come there as a farm-hand, he was a stranger. In the winter he chopped wood for charcoal. Getting on for forty he was, and unmarried; he seemed rather meditative and had coal-black hair and brown eyes like those the Lundgrens of Granträskliden always have. In the summer he had dug a well for the Holmgrens. It was twenty-five feet deep and he dug it without help and it has never run dry. That's what he was like. And I remember that we sang: "Oh, thou bitter well of sorrow, oh thou wretched sinful body, how shall our hearts thee satisfy."

He sat over by the pantry door, behind all the others, he sat looking down at the floor. And I looked at him and thought: "He only wants company for a while, he does not look like a man who wants salvation."

But when all the others had gone – they went quietly and carefully, their souls were bowls of the waters of life – he sat where he was by the pantry door. And I went up to him.

And I remember that I said: "Are you longing to clothe yourself in the garment of salvation?"

Then he looked up and looking up at me said: "If only it was enough to long."

"But it is still a beginning," I said.

"I can see redemption before me," he said. "But I shall not be able to enter therein."

He sat holding out the palms of his hands and looked at them; they were large and sort of rough.

"Our Lord has you in mind," I said. "He has everyone in mind."

And I drew up a chair and sat down beside him. "This will take time," I thought.

"I'm stuck fast in the devil's snare," he said. "The devil has his dwelling in my heart."

"Yes," I said. "It may seem like that. But it is only contrition."

"Contrition?" he said.

"Our heart is contrite," I said. "And then it feels just like the devil."

But then he said: "I am not contrite. I am calm and in full control. And I am at the height of my powers."

"He is obdurate," I thought. "The sword has not gone through his soul, he lacks the right understanding, his heart is hardened, he only knows about wood for charcoal and digging wells."

"You can't win salvation without a struggle," I said.

"If it was only that," he said and looked at his great hands. "If it was only a struggle."

"Yes," I said. "It's a matter of fighting the good fight of faith." Then I described the laws of mercy to him, the laws of mercy that men must know by heart, though in these parts it isn't common. One must never leave anything to chance.

"The call, when the Word seizes hold of you and shakes you.

"Enlightenment, when the Spirit holds out its light towards your sin.

"Regeneration, when Our Lord opens your eyes and bestows life on you once more.

"Conversion, when He fills you with His will, and helps you to forget what you yourself want.

"Righteousness, when Our Lord endows you with belief so that you become righteous.

"Sanctification, when He obliterates the sin in your heart.

46

"Steadfastness, when the Spirit holds you fast so that you don't run off in all directions.

"Blessedness, when the Spirit tells you: 'Now the struggle is over, now everything will be made clear to you.'"

"Yes," he said. "For some people it is as simple and painless as that."

"But for you the laws of mercy are impossible?" I said.

"Yes," he said. "Even if I use force I can't penetrate the laws of mercy."

"But what if you have help?" I said.

"And if you also used force?" he said.

"Where the laws of mercy are concerned one must not be considerate," I said. "It is a struggle for life or death."

"You must not be too sure," he said, and looked hard at me. "Sometimes even a preacher may be at a loss."

"Where the laws of mercy are concerned, there is no pardon," I said.

"And the meeting is over," he said. "Both the meeting and what comes after. You may need to rest. Your sermon was like a good day's work for a man."

"Nothing," I said. "Nothing I need to rest from if I can save a soul."

"And you've had no food," he said. "No evening meal."

"I can eat cold porridge," I said. "If I can save a soul I shall eat cold porridge with joy in my heart."

And then at last he told me how things were.

"I went to sea," he said. "I went to sea for four years. We plied between Holmsund and Stockholm with timber, and between Stockholm and Holmsund with earth and stones, it was called ballast. The last trip we did we had to take on board some barrels of tar in Örnsköldsvik. We stayed there for the night and I went ashore; it wasn't particularly amusing on the boat, and I was like a tall-growing sapling. I could not just lie on my back in my bunk.

"And I met a man who sold clocks and razors and silver rings.

He had schnapps and I bought a knife from him, a knife to clean my nails with. And we chatted together; he was born in Glommerträsk, so it was almost as if he came from home, and we sat ourselves down on a bench down below Strandgatan, opposite the town park; I remember it as if it was yesterday; and he said:

"'I can make clocks go backwards.'

"'Indeed,' I said.

"'You don't believe me,' he said.

"'No,' I said. 'If clocks are sound, they go in the same direction as time.'

"He had a little gold ring in his right ear and a parti-coloured neckerchief under his shirt, and his hair was black and curly; he was a bit like a gipsy, and it seemed as if he was offended that I didn't believe him.

"'The world is not as simple as North-sea-dwellers believe,' he said. 'There is more between heaven and earth than North-sea-dwellers have dreamt of.'

"'Time goes forwards,' I said. 'Therefore clocks go forwards too.'

"'For the most part that is so,' he said. 'But not always.'

"'Though if you turn round the cog-wheel,' I said, 'then it will go backwards.'

"'You think that I am a braggart,' he said. 'Some sort of cheat.'

"'I believe that God watches over the ordering of his creation,' I said."

And I said this to him as we sat there by the pantry door: "You were right. The ear shall test the words and the mouth the taste of what you want to eat. And if one has doubts about God's laws, then one has doubts about God too."

We were quite alone in the big kitchen, it was the middle of summer so the Holmgrens were living in the bakehouse; the people who had been at the meeting were down by the bridge, chatting.

And Lundgren, the man who was born in Granträskliden and

who had been at sea and whom I was fighting to save, he continued:

"Then that clock-trickster in Örnsköldsvik took out a watch from his inside pocket. And he held it out to me and said: 'Take this.'

"And I took the watch, and he told me to examine it, that it was going as it should and that he had not turned round the cog-wheel and that the watch-case was sound and that it was wound up properly.

"It was a pocket watch and it was called Norma, and it was saying a quarter to eleven in the evening and I held it against my ear and it ticked and went so that the case tinkled good and proper.

"And he said: 'Hold it out on the palm of your hand.'

"And I did.

"And he held out his right hand and ran his finger backwards and forwards a couple of times over the watch without touching it, and he shut his eyes and his face twitched as if he had cramp, and he pursed his mouth and seemed to chew. It was as if he was saying something that wasn't to be heard.

"And after a bit he said: 'Look now and see what time it is.'

"And now it was twenty to eleven.

"And I said this to him: 'It has gone five minutes backwards. You've taken it to pieces.'

"'I can make it turn back when I like,' he said.

"'What did you do to the watch?' I said.

"'I adjusted it. My hands are magnetic.'

"'Magnetic!' I said.

"'Yes,' he said. 'Magnetic.'"

Now the people who had been at the meeting had gone home; they were not standing by the bridge any more; many of them had small children of course, and could not be away too long. And I thought: "It's hard for him to believe, something has happened to him that makes him unable really to believe, this fellow Lundgren. But it can't be just this business with the watch."

"No one can have magnetic hands," I said. "That would be supernatural. And the supernatural doesn't exist. Except of course where religion is concerned," I added.

"That's what I told him," Lundgren now said. "That's what I told that clock-trickster in Örnsköldsvik. 'No one can have magnetic hands.'

"'I can't help that,' he said. 'I say the same as you: no one should need to have magnetic hands.'

"It sounded as if he had mixed feelings about it. He took out the schnapps and we drank a drop, and the watch went on going backwards, very soon it was only ten thirty.

"'Do you believe me now?' he said.

"'Yes,' I said. 'I believe.'

"For I had seen it with my own eyes.

"'But I can't understand what you do,' I said. 'What the trick is.'

"'It's no trick,' he said. 'It's only some sort of miracle.'

"'Miracle?' I said. 'Only Our Lord can work those. And I can't see why He should bother Himself to do one of those with a pocket watch, they are such ordinary things. They are only springs and cog-wheels and balance wheels.'

"And then he said: 'It's not only pocket watches. If it was only pocket watches, that would be simple.'

"'Is it pendulum clocks too?' I said. 'Wall clocks?'

"But he didn't like me teasing him. He raised his head and looked at me, and his eyes were black and his mouth sort of twisted. And then he said: 'It's time itself. Time that watches must keep track of.'

"But then I said: 'No. Not time.'

"'Yes,' he said. 'Time.'

"'You blaspheme,' I said. 'Time is God's tool. Time is God's passage through the world when He creates.'

50

"'If you will lend me your watch,' he said, 'then I will turn back your time for you.'

"'Never,' I said.

"'You will go backwards down to your boat,' he said, 'and the boat will go back to Holmsund stern first, and when morning comes you will go to bed and you will again unload the boat of timber in Holmsund.'

"'And grandfather who died a month ago?' I asked.

"'They will dig him up and he will rise up from his coffin again.'

"'If you tamper with time then you are a dead man,' I said. 'He who turns back time, he has not the right to live.'"

I saw that the Holmgrens came out and stood on the bakehouse steps; they looked towards the windows of the big kitchen; they were asking themselves how long it was going to take to save that man Lundgren. After all he was their farm-hand.

"Yes," I said to him. "That was only right. He who believes he can change the course of time, he is not fit to live. He who abuses and reviles time, he is a blasphemer."

But that man Lundgren, he had not finished yet.

"'I know so little about God,' said that clock-trickster. 'But if he is like time, then he is pretty unpredictable.'

"'God,' I said, 'He is like the almanac and the heavenly bodies; without Him there is no stability or certainty.'

"'How can you know that?' said the clock-trickster.

"'That's what I've learnt,' I said. 'And that's how it's always been. That God has seen to it that there should be law and order.'

"'Give me your watch,' he said.

"'Never,' I said. 'You shall never have my watch.'

"'You don't dare,' he said.

"'Ought I to be afraid of you?' I said.

"'There is something you're afraid of,' he said. And it was not without a trace of a sneer.

"'It is called Omega,' I said. 'And I got it from grandfather when I was fifteen.'

"'Yes,' he said 'They are good watches. They are called branded watches.'

"'So they never . . .' I said.

"And I looked to see what the watch was saying, the watch he had bewitched; it was nearly ten but from the wrong direction. And he sat holding out his hand waiting for me to give him my watch. The Omega.

"'I just want to look at it,' he said. 'I won't do anything to it. You need not be uneasy.'

"'You're not going to touch it,' I said.

"He took out the schnapps again, he had it inside his coat, and he held out the bottle to me.

"'No,' I said. 'I won't have any more schnapps.'

"'Just a little drop,' he said.

"'No,' I said, 'it's night already. And my boat goes before seven.'

"'Only to let me see that you are not easily scared and cowardly,' he said. 'To let me see that you trust me. So you can let me have the Omega, if it really is an Omega?'

"'I don't trust you,' I said.

"'No,' he said, 'you don't trust anything. And you're right not to. There is nothing that is worthwhile trusting. Not a single living person. And no forces or powers.' And there was mockery in his voice.

"'You are a blasphemer,' I said. 'You refresh yourself with derision. And Grandfather would not have liked me to lend you my watch,' I added. 'If he had been alive.'

"But then he said: 'If you really believed in your creator then you would give me your watch.'

"'I fear my creator,' I said.

"'Yes,' he said. 'That may well be so. But you have understood what creation is really like, and that's why you are afraid: that creation is like the works of a watch, and can run in whichever

52

direction it pleases. It only needs someone to have magnetic hands, or for there to be something wrong with a cog-wheel or a spring or the balance-wheel. There is no thought, no intention, no meaning in existence.'

"And while the clock-trickster said this he held out his hand and tried to get at my Omega which I kept in an inside pocket; it was as if he believed that I should give way when I saw that creation was as treacherous and unpredictable as the works of a watch; and I grew as it were blinded, I grew so furious that everything went black, and my head shook and I wouldn't say a word, and my hands clenched so that I could hardly open them, it was like cramp. It was rage. I was blind, deaf and dumb with rage."

I saw that the Holmgrens had gone in and shut the door of the bakehouse; they no doubt saw that it was impossible to save this fellow Lundgren and that it would soon be night.

"Dearly beloved brother," I said, and I felt a pang in my heart, for nothing comes without love and pain, love and pain are like firewood and oil for salvation. "Beloved brother," I said, "the godless man's mouth is greedy for wrong. Punishments are prepared for those who mock and blows for the backs of madmen.

"Your rage, that was holy indignation."

But Lundgren did not hear me, he only looked at his hands, his big hands, and he said:

"And I stretched out my arms and took hold of him and lifted him up and he was as light as a puppy that you are beating; and I held him up before me with outstretched arms, and said, 'there's a devil inside you,' and I shook him so that the watches in his pockets rattled, and I saw by his mouth that there was something he was trying to say, but I heard nothing. I was just so filled up by that rage and I had no idea even of how it had sprung up in me; 'an Omega that I got from Grandfather,' I said, and that rage gave me cramp, something cut into my shoulders and at my back like a jack-knife, and I squeezed him together between my hands so that he grew blue in the face, and his head swung backwards and forwards like a rag doll's.

"Though at last I was forced to put him down. And then he began to defend himself. He lowered his head and drove it into my stomach so that I felt blood in my mouth, and he scratched my face and put his knee into my belly so that it felt as if something broke in pieces, and I had to throw up. I heard him say: 'It's you who have the devil inside you' and he kicked my legs and beat my chest with those small hands of his.

"So then I said: 'Either you or I. Either you or I.'

"And I lifted him up and carried him to one of the warehouses, it was a harbour warehouse; and I carried him before me with outstretched arms, and it was no good his screaming or kicking. 'God watches over the ordering of his work,' I said, and I sat him down by the warehouse wall, it was red brick, and I hit him with my fists so that the skin of my knuckles split.

"'You've got to learn that violation of eternal and everlasting right does not go unpunished,' I thought. And while I banged and hit him I heard the watches scrunch into pieces in his pockets."

"You were possessed by zeal," I said to Lundgren. "Sometimes we can be consumed by zeal. And one day the whole earth will be consumed by the zeal of the Lord."

"And towards the end I had to hold him up with my right hand and only hit him with my left," said Lundgren. "His legs gave way under him, and his head banged against the brick wall so that it sounded the way it does when one is chopping wood. 'God's law will last for ever and ever,' I said, and the last blow I gave was such as to tear him loose from my right hand and he collapsed like an empty sack and there was a jangling of broken watches as he tumbled down. And he just lay there.

"After a time I realized that he was dead. That I had beaten the life out of him. Then I went to the police station, I think it was just behind the church, and I told the police about it. 'I've killed a man, he's lying there by the harbour warehouse. He declared that he could make time go backwards, he said there was no law and order in God's creation, I killed him with my fists only, now he won't be able to do anything more.'"

"Yes," I said to Lundgren who was seeking salvation, "you couldn't have done anything else. No one should try to wriggle out of justice. We must wear justice like a mantle.

"But the clock-trickster was by no means entirely guiltless. He should never have said that about God and time that He has created. If he had not made fun of the order of things in the world, you would not have needed to kill him. So quite free of guilt he certainly is not.

"And you mustn't believe that you are beyond mercy just because you have killed a fellow human being.

"God's mercy has been made manifest in the salvation of all men. All flesh shall see God's salvation.

"Our Lord makes no exceptions, not even for a man-killer."

"And there was a court case," said Lundgren, and now he spoke so softly that it was almost difficult to hear him.

"They said it was murder. And I didn't contradict them. 'Unpremeditated' they said, and that was certainly true too. And one of the jurors, he was called Lindström and came from Sidensjö, he asked if I regretted it, and then I said:

"'No.'

"And then they fell sort of silent, but they did not ask anything else.

"And I got prison.

"But when everything was over, when I had got my sentence and they were taking me out of the room, then the judge came up to me, his name was Vigren and he was called the district judge; and he looked at me intently and then he said:

"'The devil that you have inside you, Lundgren, is one that you will never get rid of. The devil of arrogance and rage.'

"And I knew right away that he was speaking the truth.

"It was as if this was the final verdict. The verdict that will last for ever. That devil I have inside me, inside my breast, I shall come to have it there as long as I live. That was the real verdict. And that verdict, it is for life. So that mercy is something I can never reach. There is a verdict between me and mercy."

So that was the way things stood for this man, Lundgren. Now I knew how it was. Now was the time for the true struggle for salvation.

"That's not the way it is with devils," I said. "No human being can have the same devil in his breast for his whole life. Devils are like the birds of the air and the fish of the sea, they come and go, and go and come, they have no permanent resting place. And the human breast is like a shed of timber; it is full of cracks and holes, nothing is put there for ever. The human breast is not air-tight, the wind blows right through it."

"But I know him," said Lundgren now. "I feel that the devil of rage is within me still."

And he looked intently at me, his eyes were coal-black, it was as if he wanted to let me see that that devil was to be found in his gaze too.

I did not drop my eyes but said: "Those devils we have within us, they change from day to day, from moment to moment. It's just a matter of not becoming their slaves, but of driving them out bit by bit. The devil of envy, and the devils of adultery and rage and the devil of cunning. And the backward-looking devil and the devil of self-pity."

"The backward-looking devil?" said Lundgren.

"Yes," I said. "Backwards, that's a point of the compass at which one should not look unless one is obliged to. Except in the matter of sin, of course."

"If it were just sin," he said.

"The thing that you believe is the devil, that is only enlightenment," I said. "It is that you see your sin."

Now he said nothing for quite a long time.

56

"Are you sure of that?" he said at last.

"Yes," I said. "I am quite sure. It is like amen in church."

He looked up at me and I saw in his eyes that a light was beginning to dawn on him. And I thought: The time is come for him to have a tiny presentiment about mercy itself. "Regeneration," I said. "And that judge, that district judge, Vigren, he was known far and wide to talk nonsense. He was a braggart."

Actually, I have never heard that Vigren mentioned, I had never heard his name before, but I wanted Lundgren to know how mercy might taste. It is the Word that will save us. Or the words. It is the words that will save us.

"Everyone knew that," I said. "What he said was nothing to go by."

"Is that true?" said Lundgren, and he almost had tears in his eyes.

"Yes," I said. "It is the absolute truth. He was a drivel-monger. A leaky sieve. And a chatterbox."

"And you are certain that it was Vigren?" said Lundgren. "The district judge?"

"Yes," I said. "And that stuff about the devil, he said that to everyone he sentenced."

"Every single one?" said Lundgren.

"Yes," I said. "Without exception. Pick-pockets and illicit distillers, and poachers, and adulterers. The lot."

"Did he really say they had the devil inside them?"

"Yes," I said. "It was quite simply a bad habit he had."

And now you could see how regeneration and conversion were beginning to come to him; his hands relaxed and hung down without his bothering about them, and the skin of his face was smooth, and his shoulders sank down a trifle, almost as if he was about to experience some sort of peace; and he shut his eyes so that I should not see his tears.

But just then, just as the wind of conversion was blowing through his breast, just as the spirit of belief was touching his senses, just then I made a mistake. I said: "And that

57

clock-trickster in Örnsköldsvik. He couldn't turn back time. Time is irreversible."

It was a mistake to say this, it was like pouring water on the fire of salvation.

Lundgren's face suddenly darkened again, and he lifted up his hands and I saw that they were shaking. And he said: "You don't believe me."

And then I made another mistake. I said: "He was only pulling your leg. He had been out in the world and learnt a thing or two. It was foolish of you to take him seriously."

"Foolish?" said that fellow Lundgren.

"Yes," I said. "Foolish."

And then he said: "It is written: 'Whosoever shall say thou fool, shall be in danger of hellfire.' "

"Yes," I said. "But it is also written: 'The truth shall make you free.' That's why I am telling you the truth. Time, that God has created, always goes in the same direction and flows into eternity."

"That may be," he said, and now he was talking pretty loudly, "but that clock-trickster in Örnsköldsvik, he would have managed to turn time back if I had not done him to death."

"Never," I said. "Never time."

And I saw by the looks of him that now it was really a question of conversion; he clenched his hands so that his knuckles were white, red streaks appeared in his eyes, he straightened his back and stuck out his chest, so that the material round the buttons of his shirt crackled.

"We shall have to settle this," he said. "We must go outside and decide it all."

"Yes," I said. "We haven't any choice."

And we got up and stood for a bit facing each other; and he looked at me fixedly and said: "That is if preachers have any strength except in their tongues."

But then I said: "You don't know what strength is."

There were once some people in Lillholmträsk who believed

58

that preachers couldn't be other than weaklings. But then I took
the New Testament which was bound with leather, and I tore it
into two bits as if it had been a daily paper.

"As a result . . ."

And when we got outside there was dew on the grass and
complete quiet except for a screech owl. Then Lundgren said:
"You mustn't think I'm as easily saved as those who are just about
worn out."

We went behind the house. We did not want the Holmgrens to
hear us; we both knew that this would be long and hard, and the
Holmgrens were no longer young and needed their sleep.

First he tried to kick me in my tender parts, he jumped up and
stuck out his leg when he was in the air, it was something he had
learnt to do when he was at sea; but I too had learnt a thing or two,
so I dodged and got hold of his foot and pulled it so that he fell
backwards. But he was soon up again and now he took to his fists;
he aimed at my eyes and my throat, he knew how much I
depended on my throat, but I defended myself with the palms of
my hands and my elbows, and now and then I gave him a kick on
the shin, just to calm him down, but he hit heavily and hard so that
it hurt, and he kept his head down, so that it was impossible to get
at him, and he groaned and wailed with rage, the rage of the devil.
And no doubt that was why he did not kill me, he was as it were
wild and mad with rage, but I was calm and calculating, I knew his
intentions and plans, it was all part of the rules, and I told him so
as I took a couple of steps backwards, and held up my arms in
front of me. I told him: "No man can remove or escape God's
law," and I heard him reply with Paul, he groaned out the words
between his blows: "Thou art a whited wall and I shall smite
thee."

And I said: "Purification from sin is a fearful struggle."

Then he replied, and he hit at me without pause, and now it
was the first letter to the Corinthians: "Them that are without,
God judgeth" and his fists were like axe hammers and his arms
like the branches of a great fir-tree when there is a storm.

59

But finally I could feel his blows getting weaker and I stopped backing away from him and tried myself to strike a few blows and he was as it were taken off his guard, and I said: "Thou shalt not know what hour shall come upon thee." And he knew the Book of Revelations too, for he said: "I am no angel of Sardis' Church."

And I got in a tremendous blow in the middle of his nose so that he stopped dead and stood still, and then I quickly got hold of his arms and twisted him round so that I got behind his back, and when I had him in reverse as it were, I flung my arms round him and clasped my hands in front of his chest so that he was locked in and captured, but then he bent forward and tossed me with his back so that we both fell face down, though I did not loose my grip, one must never loose one's grip. And he kicked my shins with his heels, so that I was obliged to draw back my feet and knees, and I squeezed his chest so that I could hear he could hardly breathe; I couldn't bear the thought that he might be lost, a man like that, and we rolled about like small boys do when they fight, and as we spun round like that in the wet grass I saw that Holmgren, old Holmgren, had come out and stood there watching us, he'd come out so that there should be a witness there when Lundgren was saved; and now I summoned up my last strength, I hurled myself with my whole weight against him, and twisted him round and got him under me, and I pressed my forehead against the nape of his neck and pushed his head down on to the ground so that he could not move, and I said:

"Will you give up now, will you hand yourself over?"

But he said nothing, he didn't try to speak; and I let go with my right hand and seized hold of his wrist and pulled his arm on to his back and twisted it round half a turn and then I said:

"Are you prepared to accept mercy?"

But he remained silent; he was breathing quite horribly, so that I was obliged to twist his arm another half turn, and I waited a bit then I said: "Now you have justification within your reach, Lundgren. And sanctification. Will you give up your resistance and submit?"

Then he lay silent for quite a long time and just struggled. It was a fight for eternal life.

But later, at the end, I could feel him relaxing within my arms and giving up. "Yes," he said with his face down in the earth. "I give up, I want mercy." It was justification, he accepted the word, and I heard old Holmgren shouting "Allelluia". Lundgren grew suddenly limp and lifeless, like a sleeper, it was reconciliation that was filling him, the peace that suffuses a human being when the Spirit of salvation is blown into his soul and the law of mercy begins its work.

# Gloria

The Nicanors had lived in the same way through all the years. There were eight of them. Nicanor and Althea and their children. The eldest boy, Einar, was twenty-two, the smallest girl, Agnes, was seven. After Agnes it was the end.

And people said to Nicanor: "Have you lost your strength? Only six children and you've given up already?"

They knew that he was in the habit of going to Sabina in Avabäck; she was not particular and received all and sundry. It was at the weekends.

But Nicanor he said: "I'm not so much of a devil that I fuck farmfolk."

And it became a common saying: "He who is a devil, he fucks farmfolk."

It was the horse who kept them alive; Nicanor hauled logs for the firm at Holmsund and Einar too worked in the timber forest. But the horse made use of everything the poor land gave; besides feed for the horse there were only a couple of stooks of corn; they fed a cow on meadow hay and sedge. The horse was called Gloria. The earth fed Gloria and Gloria fed the firm, and the firm fed them; everything reverts to its origins.

Nicanor was forty-six and Althea was forty-four.

They had taken over their place from one of her mother's brothers. His name was Johan and he was the foreman on a big farm on the coast. He had tuberculosis in his throat; during his last years he could not utter a word; he drank himself to death. Or perhaps it was tuberculosis; he couldn't get a single word out.

When Nicanor saw in the papers that the Tsar of Russia had

lost ten thousand horses in the battle of Mukden – they went down into the bottomless swamps, many were drowned in the river Hun, and many more had their legs shot off – the men who survived the battle always carried with them the horses' shrieks of deathly fear and pain. When Nicanor read this he said: "Now at least the Tsar of Russia will be able to feed his cows."

And then he laughed, the laugh that Althea knew very well, it was only a laugh for the moment, not for life.

In the winter of 1906 the firm bought no forest in those parts, so there was no hauling for Nicanor and no felling for Einar. All they could do was to hunt and prepare wood for their household needs; Gloria had to stand purposeless in her stable like a dummy, though of course she ate. And sometimes in the afternoons when no one needed to see him Nicanor harnessed her, and he said to Althea that a horse could not thrive by standing still, Gloria must have exercise, and trot and pull something; a horse is like a human being, and Althea knew very well that he was going to Sabina in Avabäck.

She was in no way better than Althea; she was listless and thin, she was sort of damp, there was nothing special about lying with her, he had really had greater pleasure from lying with Althea. And he wished that he could tell Althea that: "It is never mostly for fucking that I go to Avabäck. It is not really that I'm willingly unfaithful, but rather that I'm in despair, desperation gnaws at my flesh and consumes my bones; my nakedness would frighten you. You would try to comfort me, Althea.

"But Sabina in Avabäck, she can stand it."

He used to hide his head in her armpit. And then he wept. And she never asked: "Why are you crying Nicanor?"

No never. She was like the earth he lived on and the world he lived in; it was exactly as if she was asleep.

"I can't achieve anything," he said with his face in against her wrinkled skin. "Nothing ever gets better. Down, everything only

64

goes downhill. All that I do is in vain, everything I have tried has come to nothing.

"I had a go at growing oats in the little fields, but it froze.

"I wanted to go to Holmsund and get a job at the sawmill, but Althea said: 'Never'.

"I wanted to buy a new sledge on credit, but the shopkeeper, Norberg, said as Althea had done: 'Never'.

"I tried to join a team of log-drivers, but they wouldn't have me. I offered them Einar, but no.

"And I read the Scriptures and tried to convert myself, but I'm no good at it. Not like the Lundmarks of Lakaberg or the Burvalls of Storholmträsk.

"And I've taken Gloria seven times to the stallion, Johan Olof's stallion who has as much seed as the sons of Noah, but she is crazy, she is barren, Gloria.

"And now I can feel that pain is on the way, I can feel it at night, the pain is like a frost inside my skeleton; all timber hauliers get pain in the end; my whole life is like dragging a sledge uphill over ice like glass."

And she said nothing. He thought that his thin face, his pointed nose, his spear-like chin and his sharp cheekbones perhaps cut into her and hurt her sensitive skin, so he turned his head a trifle, then he continued:

"Nothing is left for me. Or will be left by me. Money and food and life just run through my fingers. I never have before me an öre, a seed of corn, a foal, a spoonful of porridge, a bit of meat or a piece of cake. This is like living without anything before you, it is intolerable, it is like a punishment. A human being must have something before him.

"Oh to have something before him!"

And Sabina, she lay quite quietly, she breathed slowly as if she slept, as if she had great riches before her.

"And my children," he said. "I have nothing for them. They are as empty-handed as the holy ones in Jerusalem, and empty-handed will they remain, they will have to sell themselves for a pittance. We have given them life, I and Althea, and life is bad and meaningless for those who are bound hand and foot, it simply runs through their fingers. There are those who have control over their lives, those who have bit and bridle and reins, those who have harnessed life.

"But to be enslaved by their life!"

And she was not moved.

"If you knew the sort of life I have lived, Sabina. There in Hundberget. Up on Avaliden. And there in Barsjöheden. And inside Granträsket. Everywhere. Sometimes I have been almost frozen to death. And my load has fallen on top of me. And I've got stuck in deep snow. And frost has covered me in timbermen's huts. And I have been without food for days on end. When life is so bad and hard the meaning must be that man is to achieve something, that there should be something over, that he shall have something before him; one doesn't live just for fun, my life can't be lived just for fun."

And he was silent for a while, as if he thought that Sabina might have something to say to him. But then he said:

"He has trampled me in excrement and valued me as equal to dust and ashes. And what have I to comfort myself with? A horse, Gloria. The firm at Holmsund. Althea."

"You mustn't demand too much for yourself, Nicanor," Sabina then said.

And later she said:

"You'd better be going now, Nicanor. Gloria is standing out in the snow getting cold. And Althea is waiting for you."

But he lay where he was for a while and thought, he tried to think out still more things he could say to Sabina in Avabäck, things that he couldn't say to Althea, but he could not manage it, only the same old words came and they proved nothing.

And Gloria. Gloria was standing outside in the cold wind and might catch the strangles.

\*　　\*　　\*

66

On Christmas day Sabina in Avabäck died, it was a stroke. Someone had provided her with schnapps, Konrad in Lakaberg. They found her out by the well. She had just got up the bucket and it had fallen over and the water had spilled all over her and immediately frozen so that she was as it were packed in by smooth ice. It was horrible to look at, but all the same in some way beautiful, like a huge jewel said Ansgarius in Lillåbäck; it was he who found her.

What was he now to do on Boxing Day?

When the holiday was over Nicanor slaughtered Gloria. They heard the shot, and then he came in and said to Einar that he needed help.

And they hoisted her up there to the beams of the portal of the barn, and they skinned her and cut her into pieces. Though the blood, he poured that out behind the little smithy, where he used to bury the dogs. But her head he could not bear to see, Gloria's head. Einar had to lay that in a box for lump-sugar and carry it to the forest. "Carry it up to Ormberget," said Nicanor, "and cover it with stones so that the foxes . . ."

Then they helped one another to carry the pieces of meat into the big trough, and it was like meat from three cows. And Althea thought of the most pitiful women of Jerusalem who had to boil their own children; and she thought of Nicanor's lusts and desires and Sabina in Avabäck, and that he was an adulterer; and it was hard for her to look at the meat. The meat. And she boiled the thighs and hind parts and put them into salty water and what was left she laid in coarse salt and placed everything out in the storehouse.

After that they had food for the whole winter and far into the spring; Althea had to cook her both long and well and she was still tough and tasted of resin; but Nicanor and Einar were of course not at work so they had nothing over, nothing to put before them; and it was as if it were quiet there at the Nicanors; they no longer talked to each other. It wasn't just that simple with Gloria, at once to mourn her and eat her up.

67

In April he was five days at timber rafting out on the ice, just enough to give him the feel of being out at work again. "I'm as stiff and clumsy as a hay pole," he said, "I feel as if I were seventy." And he had pain in his legs.

"Now there is nothing more left for our Lord but just our bodies, and our stomachs cleave to the earth."

And he thought: "But of course the old words that we have in our minds, those we have also. Though the words, the words are almost only air."

And Althea was glad in a way that he nevertheless tried to talk to her.

And Althea could not forget Gloria, she felt that Gloria was alive. She had had a confidante, not to say a sister, in Gloria.

At the time that Nicanor was still out in the forest and came home again for the weekend, the first thing she said was always: "How is Gloria?"

Now she said: "What shall we betake ourselves to without the horse?"

But Nicanor did not answer. And Althea thought: "No, I mustn't talk to him about Gloria."

Althea had a miscarriage in May: it was probably the seventh month and it would have been a girl; Nicanor buried her there behind the little smithy, he had made a wooden box for her and put wood-fibre in it.

"An unsaved soul," said Althea.

"I don't know about that," said Nicanor. "She is more saved than most people, for she is saved from life."

One day at the beginning of June, it was a Saturday and the eldest child was going to Åmträsk to dance, Althea had found bird-cherry in bloom down by the stream and brought in a twig of it; and Agnes, the smallest girl, had been given a bit of pressing-paper and had borrowed the scissors to cut out a doll from it. When Nicanor stood up by the table, he was holding on to the back of a chair, and he wasn't looking at any one of them in particular, it was as if he was looking at all of them at once, and he said:

"Now I can't stand any more. Now I give up."

They stopped dead and were quite silent and quiet, all the children and Althea. Agnes stopped the scissors and Einar put down the shoes he was greasing and Paulina stood by the stove with the curling-tongs in her hand quite still, and tears came into Althea's eyes, they saw and understood that now he was in earnest, he could not stand any more, he gave up.

"And inside my bones it was like a burning fire so that I could hardly endure the pain and was nearly undone."

After a bit he sat down again, but his face was white and what was said was said.

And they went on doing all the things they had been occupied with, really they had no desire left, but life mustn't stop must it, just because a man has given up all uncertainty and all hope, it happens every day. It was five kilometres' walk to Åmträsk for the dance; and Agnes wanted to get the paper doll finished before she went to bed; and Althea had to take out the slop-pail, they had washed themselves; and Victor, the boy who was seventeen, he had to move the buttons on Einar's old breeches so that he could wear them at the dance; and Paulina had to make her hair look pretty. Yes, they all had something they had to do, something important and pressing, but their hands could not free themselves from the words Nicanor had spoken.

And later while they were dancing in Åmträsk, both waltz and schottische, and polka, and while they sweated and stamped, and counted the beats, they heard within them: "Now I can't stand any more, now I give up." The words had as it were taken root in their minds and filled their hearts and their blood. And Agnes slept restlessly that night, she heard those words in her sleep, and in the morning she had broken her doll by lying on it; and Althea lay awake, it was as if she were seeking a hole or a slit in this thing Nicanor had said, a gate between the words.

Though Nicanor, he at length slept the whole night through without even having to get up to pee.

"Now I can't stand any more. Now I give up."

They didn't know it, but this thing Nicanor had said was like a charge of dynamite, like a gale and cold water when it splits and splinters hot stone. You could not escape those words of his, it was necessary that they should be said, they were devastating, every one of them in Nicanor's house was wounded. Within six months they were scattered before the winds of heaven:

Einar went to Bure and in time became a sawmill hand.

Edna took a job as a maid in Noret. Or perhaps it was Sillarliden.

And Paulina was in the family way and had to get married in a hurry.

Elvina got a wasting sickness and died. It was an internal disease.

Victor made his way to Umeå and became a soldier.

And a couple in Avafors, they were called Nordström, took charge of Agnes. When she was newborn they had said that if things went to pieces for the Nicanors they would very willingly have Agnes, the smallest girl; they were childless.

And Nicanor made it known that he wanted to be rid of the place, the place he had taken over from Johan who had tuberculosis in his throat, and in August they actually managed to sell it to an old couple from Lakaberg, a brother of Konrad's. He had been a tailor, and "every man who has abandoned his house shall get a hundredfold back," said Nicanor.

And so in the autumn they went to America. They challenged America with Nicanor's words. Nicanor and Althea, and they didn't have anything beside what they stood up in, they had shared out the little they had among the children, into the bargain they had sold their wedding rings.

70

The ship they travelled with was called the Sabina, and Nicanor said that that name, it was probably a good omen.

"Though I should be glad if she had been called something else," said Althea. "Whatever you like, Gloria."

# Merab's Beauty

This you shall know, all created things are unfathomable.

We all have the same spirit, yet most remarkable of all are the cows. No other living things are so filled with spirit and life, their udder that is weighed down by its sap and fruitfulness, and their bellies which compass four stomachs, and within all four there is life; and their eyes that understand and forgive almost everything, and their hides that tremble with happiness. Cows, they have been clothed with spiritual power.

So it was not to be wondered at that he grew despairing when his cows were not left in peace, but came back from the forest with their rumps slashed to pieces.

Gabriel Israelsson was then fifty. He was an old bachelor and had inherited the place after Conrad his father. He had never had any brothers and sisters. He was sort of dried up and solitary – even as a child he was a weakling, and he lost his teeth before he was thirty. He turned his toes out and was a hunchback, and he had unnaturally long arms and his neck was long and crooked and sat as it were in front of his chest.

But his cows, all four of them, they were as beautiful and plump as cherubs, they were the most thriving cows in Lakaberg, they were called Merab, Michal, Tahpanes, Bashemath.

And people said that Gabriel Israelsson had unnatural relations with his cows, that he loved them too extravagantly, but it was not true. Sometimes in the winter, though, he slept with them – cows are like bake-ovens and chimney walls: it is as if they had a delightful shimmering glow inside them. And he talked to them and told them what it said in the papers, and it happened sometimes that he told them about his life, and wept about it with them, for what was he to do? This was especially so with Merab. With Merab in particular.

But no one can maintain that this was unnatural.

Once he had had to slaughter a cow called Rizpah – she had broken both her front legs in the big ditch over by Gransjöväg. And no one who was not related or was a stranger was allowed to touch her. He flayed her and cut her up and salted and preserved her in glass bottles. Then he took everything, all that was Rizpah, and went to the parson at Norsjö.

"Cows are not holy to us," said the parson. "They are so among heathens in the land of India."

"But all the same," said Gabriel.

So that time the parson had to give way. And after all it was a whole cow.

The first time that Bashemath came home from the forest in the evening with a stiff rump because she had had a blow on the top vertebra of her tail, Gabriel thought it must be some inanimate object that was the cause, a branch from a tree or a stake that had fallen on her.

Or perhaps an unknown cow who had ridden her.

But later when the same happened with Michal, he saw and understood what had happened, that it was a human being and not some dead object, that it was pure iniquity and ill will.

But what can a poor, solitary fellow do against man's wickedness?

For two days he kept them shut up in the cowshed and gave them last year's hay. But they thought only of the sweet grass round the cool spring over by Lidmyran; it was July and they were furious and mooed continuously. And their stiff tail-ends were full of muck, they could not lift them as they usually did, and Gabriel had to wash them with soapy water.

"If only I knew who it was," he said. "Who can outrage life in

74

this way? I'd give him a going over with my sheath-knife, I'd cut him up, he has no right to live."

But on the first day he let them out again it was Tahpanes who got her rump slashed.

And while he washed her and rubbed her dry with a sackcloth towel he thought: "It is someone who has no feeling for the dignity of life. Someone whose heart is blind. But Merab he shall not touch. Not Merab."

So the next day in the morning he took his fowling-piece and followed the cows into the forest: they walked before him rocking from side to side; here and there they rested by some tussock. Merab went last, she was heavy with confidence and the joy of life, the muscles under her skin moved like waves of water and her udder swayed like a hanging cradle, her beauty was almost like a pain inside him.

"Merciful God!" thought Gabriel.

He had a bit of smoked meat in his pocket, and when Merab, Michal, Tahpanes and Bashemath stood still in some good place, he sat himself on a stone and cut himself strips of meat.

Merab's back and sides were black, her cheeks were white and up on her thighs she had stars, white stars, and her ears had white edges and between her eyes there was a light-coloured tuft; she was the most beautiful cow he had ever seen.

Beyond Lidmyran, this side of the cool spring, Quaking-grass spring, they stopped for the day; first they ate then they lay down and ruminated, after that they ate again, they did not guzzle, but grazed thoughtfully and heartily; Gabriel sat in the shade under that big pine tree you know, at the back of the spring up in the forest; sometimes he cut off a bit of meat, three times he went to drink; smoked meat is salt.

When evening began to fall they stationed themselves at the edge of the bog and looked towards Lakaberg – Merab and Michal and Tahpanes and Bashemath. They ruminated and thought about the homeward journey; they thought through the paths and coppices and the charcoal-burners' sites they had to cross, and the big ditch before Gransjövägen.

And then they began to walk; it was the best part of an hour's way. Bashemath went first and Gabriel reflected that he must buy her a bell, a brass bell, she was in essence a bell-cow, she had in her the spirit of wisdom.

But she was no beauty like Merab.

He walked fifty paces behind them; in his right hand he carried his fowling-piece. He saw that the berries would soon be ripe. Now on their homeward journey the cows did not indulge in any rests spent eating a tuft of grass for fun; they walked calmly and wisely in a file as if bound together by a rope. "Today they will be left in peace," he thought. "Today I have saved Merab from having her rump slashed to pieces."

Though that was something he should not have thought.

There by the charcoal-burners' sites, the charcoal areas where Erik Granström usually had his charcoal stacks, just when Bashemath had got so far that she only had cinders under her hoofs, just at that moment a man stepped out from behind the charcoal-burners' hut, the little black hut that Granström had always had there, and he had a spruce stake in his hand.

And Gabriel saw straightway who it was, he recognized him immediately, he could not avoid instantly seeing and knowing who it was; he ought to have been able to work out long before who it was.

He was a big fellow and thickset and his belly hung over his belt; he had a sunburnt, shining red face, and he was wearing black trousers and a striped grey waistcoat which he had always worn, and the little finger of his right hand was missing – that finger had been cut off when he and a man from Lycksele had fought with lifting pikes at the timber-floating. That missing little finger was something Gabriel remembered better than any other fingers God had made.

And he gazed at the cows, he only had eyes for the cows. Gabriel he did not see.

Now even Merab had reached the cinders, she was swishing her tail to drive away the mosquitoes. She was full of food and absent-minded and unmilked.

Then he lifted up that spruce-stake as if it had been an axe or a leaching club and ran towards her, towards Merab. He said nothing, but his mouth was wide open as if he were trying to shout but couldn't. He was possessed and mad; he aimed with the spruce-stake at Merab's rump. Oh merciful Lord!

Gabriel did not touch his gun, it hung on his right hand, but what use was it? Now that he had seen who it was.

But just when the spruce-stake had reached its highest point, just when it had begun to fall towards Merab, towards her rump, he at last came to himself. He drew the deepest breath of which he was capable and tensed his throat so that it was as still as a stove-pipe and he yelled, yelled so that it could certainly be heard over the whole of Lakaberg, yes even over in Mörken:

"Old Dad! Old Dad! Don't!"

And his father stopped in the middle of a step and in the middle of a blow and stood still as he usually had done when things didn't go as he had intended. And Merab behaved as if nothing had happened, she wanted to get home to Lakaberg, she was unmilked.

It is no use shooting at a ghost who walks again.

Or to talk to it?

For a long time they stood staring at each other, they kept watch on each other like two bull calves; how can anyone find his enemy and let him escape? And the cows went on their way and could no longer be seen between the trees.

He looked just as he had done when alive, plump, not to say bloated, his eyes were flecked with red, his trouser legs were tight over his thighs and his hands were broad and hairy; in his nostrils he had hairs and on the hairs hung drops of water.

77

They had in fact never been able to talk to each other.

But at last Gabriel said: "So old Dad, you're haunting us are you?"

But Conrad did not answer.

And now Gabriel recalled what had happened when he died, how he had parted from life.

He had been lying on the maidservant in her bed – they kept a maid at that time – in his right hand he held his gold watch and he had crushed it, whether from lust or from a stroke it was impossible to say, he had the stroke as he lay on the girl, and with his left hand he had dug into her breast, so that they had to bandage her afterwards.

"Signe, the maid you lay with, she now lives with Zadrak in Nyklinten," said Gabriel. "They have two children."

Then his face twitched, old Dad's face; it looked as if that pricked him, but he did not say anything.

"You are quite like yourself," Gabriel said. "You haven't changed."

And then at last Conrad opened his mouth. "That is probably true," he said. "The only difference is that I am not alive."

"Though you haunt instead," said Gabriel.

"Yes," said Conrad. "But that is a weak futile comfort,"

"He has forgotten the cows," thought Gabriel. "I must get him to think of something else. It's a matter of finding the right words, those that are as slippery as butter, words that are like deep water; the cows have still a long way to go." Words, though, had never been his strong point. Even if he felt he had them inside him, he could never get them out.

"Have you ever found out why you are haunting in this way?" he said at last.

"No human being knows why he is alive," said Conrad. "And no ghost knows why he walks either."

If Bashemath had had a bell, a brass bell, then he would have been able to hear how far they had got, then he would have known when they were far enough off, when they stood still by the gate the bell would have remained silent.

"Is it because of the evil in you that you can't be at peace?" he said.

"I wasn't more evil than others," said Conrad, and he sounded cocksure as he had always done.

"Evil tasted delightful in your mouth," said Gabriel.

"It was the taste of life I wanted to have in my mouth," said Conrad.

"You beat us children," said Gabriel. "With the cane grandfather left you. And you killed the kittens with your fingers because it gave you pleasure. You stole bundles of wood from Anton's Hanna. You lay with the maidservants though they were unwilling. You always wanted to have six cows though you only had hay for five. Your evil cunning made you always deadly enemies with your neighbours, and you said time after time that you would kill shoemaker Dalin, so that he lived in fear all his life. And you shut Mother up in the little chamber in the loft so that she went more or less mad."

"The maids were willing enough," said Conrad. "And I shut Mother up so that I could be sure of keeping her."

And he pursed his lips and chewed as it were, so that the muscles in front of his ears moved in and out; and Gabriel recognized that too.

"He who purses his lips, he bringeth evil to pass," said Gabriel.

That was from the Book of Proverbs.

But then Conrad said: "Cursed be he who curses his father."

That was the Book of Deuteronomy.

Then Gabriel lost his temper and he said: "I ought to have killed you. I ought to have killed you while you were still alive."

"You weren't man enough for that," said Conrad. And he looked contemptuously at Gabriel, his son. He was thin and crookedly built, he looked like a post and like dried fish. "If you used both your hands you could not straighten out my forefinger," said Conrad.

79

"Evil has no limits," said Gabriel.

"But it is not infinite," he added.

"What you call evil is simply life itself," said Conrad. "That to which you give the name evil, that is what is quite natural."

And what answer could Gabriel give to that? He would have needed the word that was the only right one, he had to search for it, that was what he was searching for all the time. And he thought: "Is there a word that is so strong and corrosive that it dissolves those who haunt?"

And Conrad said: "It is this hunger. It is as if I have never been able to eat enough."

"You were never a moderate eater in the matter of life," said Gabriel. "But now you are no longer in the flesh, old Dad."

"That's what is so damnable," said Conrad. "I long to be back in the flesh."

And when he said this his face twitched again as if he had a pain inside him.

"The senses of the flesh are death," said Gabriel.

"No," said Conrad. "Life, that is to have a sense of the flesh."

"Now they will soon be home," thought Gabriel. "Now Merab, Tahpanes, Michal and Bashemath are in safety for this time." And he began to cross the charcoal-burning site on his way home.

"You have never understood the flesh," said Conrad, who was walking a few steps behind Gabriel. "You have never understood how to take advantage of the joys of the flesh."

Gabriel wouldn't dispute that; the joys of the flesh. How is one to know what the joys of the flesh are, or what Joy is?

"Is it the joys of the flesh that make you unable to leave the cows in peace?" he said.

Conrad didn't answer immediately; they were walking through the dwarf birch scrub down by Gårdmyran; there were unripe cloudberries.

At last he said: "I can't bear to look at them. And yet I can't let be, they tempt me with some unknown power. I hate them. And

80

they are so well formed and handsome that I could weep when I see them."

"Yes," said Gabriel. "He who knows how to behold a cow, he does not need to look at anything else in the world. He need never have thirsty eyes again."

"Yes," said Conrad. "It is unreasonable that living creatures should be allowed to be as perfect as they are. It is intolerable."

"Their hair is like silk," said Gabriel. "If I knew what silk was like. And their udders are like women's breasts, but more mighty, and they never go dry. And their heads that are so full of thoughts that they bow low with every step they take. And their tails that move like butterflies, no human beings have an ornament like that."

"Yes," said Conrad. "The tail is probably the worst."

"On the day of judgement cows will be placed on the right hand of the Lord," said Gabriel. "But you will be standing on the left hand among the goats. The cows, they are like God's daughters."

"They are so full of life," said Conrad. "The very sap of life, and it makes me furious when I see them."

"And then you feel obliged to hit them?"

"Yes. Then I am forced to hit them."

"Over their rumps?"

"Yes, over their rumps."

And Gabriel was still seeking for the right word. When he happened to see a ripe cloudberry he bent down, picked and ate it, and he thought: "*He* can't do that. He can't eat cloudberries."

"And so it is a sort of jealousy," he said.

"Because they bear the beauty of life."

"Yes," said Conrad. "It is like jealousy."

Perhaps it was that the right word did not exist? Perhaps the right word against the misery of death, its need and its anguish was not a word of the sort that the mouth can utter?

And yet he was all the same almost like a living being, was old Dad.

And they kept something like company together.

"It's frightfully hard luck on you, Dad old man," he said.

And when they had nearly reached the big ditch before Gransjövägen, Gabriel said: "You mustn't chastise life. You mustn't hit at it with spruce-stakes. You must hold it dear."

And when they got up to the ditch he said the last words just as he was jumping over Gransjöväg ditch, so that he blew a number of words over the ditch out into the air as he jumped, and it sounded as if these words were greater than the others, and the greatest was compassion.

"Love manifests itself only for those who feel compassion for everything in life. Compassion and love, they are what shields us from eternal death."

And he heard the old man, old Dad, take a run at the ditch behind him, and he heard him stamp and jump, and make the leap. But he never landed.

Only the spruce-stake was left, and Gabriel picked it up and took it home for firewood.

Perhaps he had in the end found the right word? Though which it was he was never able to decide. He had said so many words, so horribly many. But perhaps this about the cows being God's daughters.

They stood there by the gate mooing, Merab and Michal, and Tahpanes, and Bashemath. And he could hear quite clearly which voice was Merab's.

And when he had milked them and when he had fed them, only a little evening supper, and watered them, he was up half the night in the smithy, he hammered out a sort of shield out of plate-metal, an iron guard to fix firmly to Merab's lumbar regions and her topmost tail vertebra; for all created things are imponderable and you can never be too sure, and no human words last for ever. They lose their power.

And towards morning he lay down to sleep for a while beside Merab. She lay ruminating the grass she had found there at the

Quaking-grass spring, and inside her belly it sounded as it does in the forest in spring, buds and melted snow and weather as of yore.

"Can you understand?" he said to her. "My old Dad. That old dead Dad. All the same, can you understand it?"

# Two Letters

# Water

To the County Council at Umeå.

There is water that is cold and dense as stone, you cannot drink it, and there is water which is so thin and weak that it does not help if you drink it, and there is water that shudders when you drink it so that you get the shivers; and there is water that is bitter and tastes of sweat; and some water is as it were dead, water-spiders sink down through it as if it were air. Indeed water is like the sand on the shores of the sea, its numbers are countless.

So that the form which you, the County Council, have sent us to enable us to tell you what our water situation is, that is useless, there isn't room for water in two lines. If you have lived for seventy years as I have done, then you will know so much about water that the whole County Council could drown in that knowledge.

So I cannot say everything.

When we moved up here to Kläppmyrliden we bought the place from Isaac Grundström, they had six children and thought it was too cramped. Theresa and I had of course no children, we had been married more than five years, Isaac Grundström was going to move to Bjurträsk and begin work at the sawmill – that was when we were cheated over water.

We were here in March and viewed the house, and we asked: "What about water?"

"Yes," Isaac Grundström said. "We have always had water."

And they went with us out to the well – the path was covered with snow – it was behind the cowshed; and he sent the bucket down, it was pretty deep, twenty-five feet he said, and we could hear the bucket hitting water, and at that he jerked the chain so that the bucket filled and then he wound it up, and there was clear water though perhaps a trifle yellow. And I took a scoop and tasted it.

"Yes," I said, "though it has a smoky smell. And tastes of air. It can't be denied that it reminds one of water from melted snow."

And then he took the scoop and drank.

"It tastes of rock," he said. "You can tell that it is water from a well."

"Yes," I said. "Or water that has pushed up through the ice."

"No," he said. "Water from a well."

Though why should we quarrel about water? There was water after all, so I said:

"Water never tastes the same to two people."

"No one has ever complained about the water here in Kläppmyrliden," he said.

"This thing about water is a sort of habit," I said. "When you have drunk a certain water for a time, then your body is full of that water. And after that you can no longer tell its taste."

So we bought Kläppmyrliden.

But the first winter we lived here, about Candlemas it was, the well was dry.

And we asked people, the neighbours: "How can it be that the well is empty? When we were here last year to look at the place, then there was water. And Isaac Grundström said that it never ran dry."

"That well, that runs dry every winter," said the neighbours. "And some dry summers."

And into the bargain they said: "That was why Isaac Grundström moved. It was because of the water."

"Though last year there was water," I said.

"Never," they then said. "But Isaac Grundström knew that you would ask: 'What about water?' So they filled up the well ready for when you came; they melted snow in the wash-tub, they worked for three days with the water, they carried it in buckets out to the well, Isaac and Agela and all the six children."

"So they filled the well with melted snow?" I said.

"Yes."

"That's how we were cheated."

Though in fact I understood him, Isaac Grundström, he would not have been able to sell Kläppmyrliden if he had said: "The only trouble is that the well runs dry every February;" and of course he had to get the place sold.

But things went well for us; we were only two, me and Theresa.

I tried at first with the cold well at Kläpp, it was only a few kilometres up in the forest, and I thought, we can very well carry the water, and I hacked and bored down through the ice, but the ice ended in moraine earth, it was frozen solid to the bottom.

After that there was nothing for it but to carry snow and melt it in the wash-tub. It was a trifle yellow and had a sort of smoky smell and tasted of air.

And I said: "Come the summer I shall dig that well a few feet deeper."

And that's what I did. In May we got our water back, before midsummer we bailed the well dry and I nailed together a twenty-five-foot ladder so that I could get down and then I dug, I dug down two feet for sure and Theresa helped me by winding up what I dug loose, it was hard-packed earth consisting of sand, clay and gravel, and water came, so much so that it was nearly impossible to dig. And I said: "Now we shall never need to be without water again."

And that year we managed right up to the first Sunday in Lent. But then it dried up. After that we had to melt snow until Holy Week when the water came up through the ice.

Otherwise it was good water, the water that was in the well, smooth and clear though a trifle sweet.

And when summer came again I dug once more.

It wasn't particularly hard to dig, an iron bar and a spade was all I needed. And things were just the same now as in the previous summer, it ran so that I was standing in water the whole time though Theresa bailed me out bit by bit.

But after that I came down to rock, real primitive rock, I'd only dug down a foot. And I thought "that's the end now. But I might as well dig it clean, I'll clear the rock so that the bottom of the well is like a sitting-room floor," and I dug with my hands so that not a fistful of sand or clay should remain, but as I did it the rock felt like ice to my hands. So there must be a hole somewhere, just like the cracks you find in sea-ice. I had the bad luck to open that crack so that the water I had round my feet ran away, the well was dry in a moment, it even sounded as if the rock was sucking up the water, the noise it made was the same as you make when you pull a cork from a bottle, and not even as much as dew was left.

But Theresa said: "It's not your fault. When it's a matter of depth no one can know what it is just right to dig."

After that we were entirely without. And I had not time to dig any more that summer.

Summer is as short as a shooting-star.

That winter we took water from the cold spring at Kläpp, and when the frost got into the ground then we melted snow in the cauldron that was used for the big wash.

I made a yoke for Theresa so that she could carry two buckets. I formed it to fit her shoulders and neck so that it should not cause her unnecessary pain and produce sores, and Theresa said it was a blessing, that yoke.

If only we had had children they could have carried water.

But neither of us said anything about that. We were unable to have children; the yoke of barrenness is hard to bear. It was hardest for Theresa.

When summer came again I dug over by the wood-shed. Theresa stood and pulled up the buckets of earth; I dug down eighteen feet, when I was down to the rock, but there was not a drop of water, the moraine earth was not even damp.

And I said to Theresa: "This damned hump. This dry heap of gravel, this is like the Desert of Sin."

"Though the Scriptures speak of the 'springs of great depth'," said Theresa.

"Yes," I said. "But how to find them."

"Yes," she said. "'The springs of great depth, they are hidden', it also says that in the Scriptures."

"It will be the death of me, this water," I said.

"It isn't the water," Theresa then said, "it is quite the other way round."

"But when summer comes I shall dig again," I said, "then I shall dig a bit below the old well, there must be water there."

"Yes," said Theresa. "For water is sure to be somewhere. It's only hidden like the good wine at the wedding in Cana."

And there was water, an absurd amount of water. I began to dig the first week in June and by the third day we could not bail any longer. Theresa was quite done in, I had got straight down to a vein of water, it was in sand and we said: "Now we shall have water for at least as long as we live, this well will never dry up. So at least there'll be water."

And it was only ten foot deep.

But water must be given time to clear, there is always sediment when it is newly dug, sludge and mud and earth. "The well must be given a couple of days, but then we shall never be without water," we said. "And we will thank Our Lord for this single thing, that we have at last been given water."

Though of course we had a trial tasting.

And we said: "No, it still has too much of an earthy taste."

But after a week had gone by it was still not clear, it was yellowish brown and on the surface it shimmered like a rainbow, and we were obliged to say: "No it doesn't taste of earth, it tastes of iron, though it will do for the animals," we said.

But not even the cows could bring themselves to drink it, they seemed to be alarmed and bellowed loudly and flung their heads about when we put it out for them, so there was nothing for it but to fill in the new well and I had not time to dig any more that summer; and I remember that we had got a stillborn calf, and I put him in the bottom and then filled it in; what good has a man for all his toil, it was nothing but a sort of grave-mound over the calf.

That winter we thought "at last!" Theresa was certain in October; she was sick and couldn't bear any food but salt pork, and I said it was like a miracle – it was like when Moses struck the rock with his staff. We were anxious, and we rejoiced, it was even so that I helped her to carry water though the neighbours said: "Oh indeed, since when has it been a man's job to carry water?"

But in December she had a miscarriage, she was carrying snow down to the wash-tub and it seemed as if something burst behind in her back.

She recovered quickly, though; she has always been strong, has Theresa, if I hadn't had Theresa, I don't know. . . . And it wasn't anyone's fault, how could anything be anyone's fault?

Then in the winter, in February, I heard someone mention a well-digger in Strycksele who was called Johan Lidström, he usually went about with his rod and he never made a mistake, and when he had pointed out the place, he dug, and if there wasn't water he would never take any money.

So I sent a sort of message with Andreas Lundmark – he was going to Strycksele in any case when he went to Vindeln – and I sent my greetings to that man Lidström and told him that we were not quite satisfied with the water up at Kläppmyrliden, and that we certainly should not say no to his help if he thought he had time.

On the Monday after Whitsun he came. He was tall and thin and had a bit of a hump – perhaps it was the digging – and he was deplorably cocksure and pretty nearly arrogant, he seemed to be a sort of water doctor.

I told him what had happened to us in the matter of water.

"Now we've been living here for seven years," I said. "Without water. And I really have dug. I've dug so that I've more or less got a hump on my back."

I wanted us to understand each other.

"You have only dug haphazardly," he said. "You've fumbled like a blind man in the dark."

"Not so," I said. "I've dug as wisely as any man. You can see for yourself all the places where I've tried to dig."

"Water is strange," he said. "It is inscrutable. It is a sort of science."

"True," I said. "And you can't live without it."

"Ordinary people should never have a go like this with water," he said. "Those who haven't got the right insight."

"When one is without water then one digs in desperation," I said.

"It's never worthwhile to dig in desperation," he said. "Water does not bother itself about people who cry and complain. You can't take water by surprise."

"But you may come right to a vein of water. Like a trick of fate."

"Yes," he said. "And that's almost the worst of it. Veins of water are as touchy as a child's eye. Veins of water are as fragile as a mirage. People simply destroy veins of water when they dig."

"But you, you never make a mistake," I said. "For you things never go wrong over water."

"Never," he said. "I've learnt to take water seriously. Streams of water in the earth, they are like the veins of blood in the human body."

And he added: "The King and Parliament should write a law about water. To prevent people digging just anyhow. And they say the world goes forward! I am convinced," he said, "I am convinced that sooner or later they will be obliged to write such a law. Digging a well, that is like putting a child into the world. Life and water, they are one and the same thing."

And he really took pains, he spent a lot of time, for two days he walked about first spying out the land. He examined the grass, he lifted up the turf and smelt the earth, he went about with his rod – it was of fresh birch – and he crept about on all fours and felt his way with his fingers and he lay down on his stomach and kept quite still, he said he could sometimes hear the water bubbling in the ground, he jabbed with his iron pole and pushed pieces of wood down into the holes. He wanted us to see how remarkable it was, this business with water, that it was knowledge and art.

At last, on the morning of the third day, he said:

"This is the place, it is here I shall dig."

It was behind the wood-shed, where the raspberries are, it is mostly only gravel there.

"Twenty feet," he said. "Twenty feet, but then you will have water for the whole of your life, and the children and descendants you have unto the third and fourth generation."

"I will do the roughest digging," I said. "Just the top bit. Before we get down to the water itself. I don't want to injure the vein," I said.

"No," he said, "I shall dig all of it. It is the beginning of a thing that decides the end."

And indeed he was a capable well-digger. He did not move fast but all the same he was clever. I sat myself down in the barn doorway and mended the rakes, and in between whiles I took a turn and stood beside him, it was as if he sank into the ground, a foot an hour.

And when he got down so far that only his head was visible I took the pail and helped him to heave up the earth, little by little; he was very careful about the corners and he dug square not round.

And I said to him: "I have always dug round wells. Not square."

"Yes," he said. "I know. People dig round wells. They believe that you must dig them round."

We had to get up a couple of stones with the stump-grubber. And I said to him that it was a lucky thing they were not firmly stuck in the soil.

"I knew that," he said. "I never dig where there are stones stuck fast in the soil."

When Saturday evening came, he had dug seventeen feet. He had a thing like a plummet to measure the depth.

"By Monday," he said, "by Monday, then we shall come to water. Then you will see a stream."

He was there over the whole of Sunday, he kept close to the well, but he did not dig, he walked about half kicking the earth, and now and then he sat on the mound of earth, he sat and thought.

But Theresa, she said to me on Sunday evening: "Do you think he'll find water?"

"Yes," I said. "He seems so sure."

"I don't believe he'll ever find a vein," said Theresa. "He is too insolent. He's nothing but arrogance."

"If you've hunted up as much water as he has done, you have the right to be arrogant," I said.

"I believe that the man who can find water, he must be humble," said Theresa. "He must have something like love."

And I remembered how I had dug for all those years and found not a drop.

"You mustn't be superstitious," I said. "Either there is water or there isn't. And I believe in him."

At dinner time on Monday, he had dug twenty feet and I called and asked: "Do you see any water, Lidström?"

"Not quite yet," he answered. "It may be I am short by a few inches."

But when we had eaten and came out again and he climbed down, why it was just as dry at the bottom as when we went in.

And he called to me. "I'll take out a few spits more."

And he continued to dig.

If by chance the County Council really want to know what has happened to us in the matter of water.

\*    \*    \*

When he had dug twenty-five feet – that was on Tuesday, I wrote it down in the calendar – then I called down to him for the first time: "I don't believe there's water in this place."

But he called back: "I'm quite sure there's water. And I won't give up."

So there was nothing for it but to stand there and take the buckets he filled down in the well; and I felt it with my hand and there was only dry gravel in them. And Theresa came out and stood beside me and I said to her: "It's dry gravel, nothing else."

And then she said: "It's almost worse for this man Lidström. You and I can manage, we are not spoiled in the matter of water. But I don't think he can endure this disgrace."

"So you believe him," I said. "You believe that he has never in his life been mistaken in the matter of water?"

"Yes," she said. "I believe him. Poor man."

"He need not have been so dead sure and so big for his boots," I said. "Even if he usually has luck about water."

"We must think of some way to comfort him," said Theresa. "Kidney-blood pudding. I'll go and cook some kidney-blood pudding."

"Yes," I said. "For he'll never get any money for this dry well."

And I was having to nail new rungs to the ladder all the time.

He didn't eat kidney-blood pudding. He couldn't endure the smell, he said.

When he had got down thirty-five feet, I asked him: "Won't you soon be down to the rock?"

But he answered: "There are ten feet left before I get down to the rock. And on top of the rock there will be water."

But all the same it seemed as if he was a trifle melancholy, when we ate and when we drank our coffee he said never a word, and he went to bed immediately after our evening porridge; he slept up in the attic.

On Thursday morning, though, just as he was about to climb down into the well again, he said: "This is serious. There are those who dig wells as it were at random. But for me it is a serious business."

And you could see that this was the truth.

But when I could see by the lead-line that it was now forty-two feet, I called down to him: "Lidström, this is absolutely futile. Now you must stop."

But he answered, and it was difficult to hear him, forty-two feet is deep down in a well: "Only a few inches more. Or a foot. Then there will be water."

But I called: "You deceive yourself. You deceive yourself. This patch is as dry as the Desert of Sin."

But he called back to me: "Don't be so deadly obstinate, just go on pulling up the buckets."

And I said: "I don't give a damn for this well any more. Devil take this well."

But then he called: "Who is it who really knows about water? Is it you or I?"

And then he jerked the chain to show that the bucket was full and I pulled it up. "One foot more," I thought. "But after that it's finished, after that he must climb up the ladder himself with his buckets of gravel."

And on Saturday morning – we were just going to have our mid-morning coffee – it was forty-five feet.

"Lidström," I shouted. "Lidström. Not an inch more. Not even a grain of gravel."

But he answered: "Don't you interfere in this. I shall dig as deep as I please."

And I shouted: "You have promised to dig two more wells in Norsjö this summer."

"Yes," he answered. "But I only dig one at a time."

"But I have other things to do than to stand here heaving up buckets," I said. "I haven't got the summer left."

"When there is water," he shouted, "you'll be grateful that I didn't give up just because it was a few inches deeper than one thought."

And I could hear even up there how he continued to dig and delve as we were talking.

"But Lidström," I shouted, "don't you understand what I'm saying to you? Now there must be an end to this. Now you must come up. This is the end of the dig."

And then he called from the bottom of the hole where he was which was perhaps the deepest well in the Norsjö district:

"You can't order me about. I shall dig as much as I please. I have my freedom. I am a free human being. And a free human being digs as long as he pleases."

And it seemed as if I had no patience left. I felt I was forced to get him out, even if I had to climb down and carry him up the ladder myself.

"But the land is mine," I screamed. "The land you're digging down into. I shall decide myself if some stranger comes here and digs deep dry holes. No outsider shall try to take command over this stony ground."

And I stamped on the ground, I was so provoked, I stamped hard with my right foot on the ground.

And then there was a rumbling down in the well, it sounded like rain on a barn roof, it was the south wall of the well that gave way, it wasn't strutted, and I hastily jumped backward a few paces; the edge above the well was moving too, there was no moisture to hold the gravel and sandy soil together so it rushed and ran like the sand in an hour-glass; it was like it is when powder snow fills in a footprint in winter; the whole well disappeared as if it had been dug down in a large lake that had fallen back again into place, all that was left of the well was a sort of hollow in the ground, that forty-five foot well.

And I was powerless, wasn't I?

And I called to Theresa and she came out and we stood there a while, she had tears in her eyes and she said: "Think if he had to suffer."

"It went so horribly quickly," I said. "I even believe that he is still standing upright. He is standing upright at a depth of forty-five feet."

"He wanted to do his best," she said. "That was all he wanted. To do his best."

"I told him to come up," I said. "If he had done as I told him, this would never have happened."

"Yes," she said. "He was pig-headed. But perhaps they are like that. Well-diggers."

And I was obliged to betake myself to Norsjö. I wasn't quite sure how to proceed.

"He is standing upright at a depth of forty-five feet," I said to the parson. "It would take me the whole summer to dig him out again."

And the parson he turned the matter over in his mind for a bit, then he said: "At sea one commits a dead man to his eternal rest right on the spot. Those who lose their life at sea, they are not fished up from the depths to be sunk into consecrated ground. This well-digger Lidström, the man who is standing upright at a depth of forty-five feet, he is like a sailor who has drowned in his ocean."

So I returned home and shovelled back the earth into that hollow. I put back everything that Lidström had dug out, hard packed earth and dry gravel, so that it looked smooth and tidy again, and I planted some raspberry bushes there, and Theresa made a wreath out of rowan twigs, and when two weeks had passed the parson came and carried out the burial service, yes, it was called a burial service, he said when I asked if it was really necessary to say: "From earth thou comest, to earth shalt thou return." And he had been told by the parson on Vindeln that this Lidström had no family nor any kinsfolk in Strycksele, he was a recluse of sorts, and the parson read the verse about water from Matthew: "And whosoever shall give to drink unto one of these little ones a cup of cold water, he shall in no wise lose his reward."

And Theresa said to the parson: "He assured me that he had dug over a hundred."

Nevertheless we were still without water.

And I said to Theresa many times: "If there was only one person who did not mind about water, then we would sell Kläppmyrliden to that person. But we are stuck with Kläppmyrliden."

But Theresa she said that we only need take one day at a time, we only need carry as much water from Kläppkallkällan or melt as much snow in the wash-tub as we need for the day. And we are only two aren't we?

"We are only we two."

But I said: "Think of our old age, Theresa. Who will then carry water for us? And melt snow?"

And she had to admit that I was right.

So I went on digging in various places though I knew it was in vain. I dug down into the dry gravel and the moraine earth; it was as if I felt obliged to dig a dry hole every summer. Dry gravel is like a colander for water, it's like a sieve and a tub without a bottom.

Our neighbours all had water. In Lakaberg and Inreliden and Böle and Avabäck and Åmträsk, yes even where they had water, people keep a sharp eye on those who haven't got water. And we were a childless couple who didn't have water, so that . . .

We were like Kläppmyrliden.

And Kläppmyrliden, it was like the Desert of Sin. Life, too, has an incurable drought.

After fifteen years had passed since the summer Lidström was with us – yes, that's what we said though he was actually with us still – the fifteen summers so to say, it was an unbearably dry summer and I was standing down by the small spruces of the barn sharpening the hay-poles. Then Theresa came out of the house carrying the coffee-basket, she had a bonnet on her head and was wearing a big apron, her baking-apron.

And we were no longer young, I was fifty-eight and she was fifty-seven.

I wouldn't tell everyone this. But I will tell the County Council the truth. Since the County Council have asked about water.

And we didn't have intercourse any longer, that intercourse that man and wife usually have, we hadn't strength left for everything, and dragging ourselves along up at Kläppmyrliden had taken it out of us. And besides it was in a way futile.

We sat down on the grass, she had baked a sponge-cake and she had brought out a jug of fresh water and I drank the water and looked at her and saw how wrinkled she was and how grey-haired, and that her cheekbones were much sharper than they had been and that her shoulders were a bit crooked and that she had a lump on the back of her neck, it was the yoke. And I thought: "Perhaps I should take time off and make a new one for her, one that lies like a shawl round her neck."

And it was as if she heard my thoughts for she said: "I've been thinking about the water. Whether we have been too zealous about water. So that the water has tied itself into a knot. If we hadn't searched for water so desperately, we might perhaps have found enough and to spare."

She has always been superstitious about water has Theresa.

But I did not say that. I did not say that to her, I just moved a bit closer and put my right arm around her, for this thing about water has always been a sort of sorrow for us; and she leaned her head against me, and we lay down there on the grass, and then we tried to do what we hadn't done for years, it was as it were unplanned.

It was an inspiration.

And then after a bit I was obliged to say: "It doesn't come for me. I can't manage any more."

But then Theresa said: "That doesn't matter. There is so terribly much one can never finish. I only wanted you to taste the sponge-cake."

Her patience is like a blessing.

And then she said: "I've got wet behind, on my back."

And I said: "It's not possible. It is as dry here as in the Desert of Sin."

"Feel me then," she said, and sat up.

And I felt with my hand. And she was as wet as if it had rained.
"You should have a try at digging in this place," she said.
"No," I said. "I'm sure I've dug in this place ten times."
"But if I beg you to," she said.

So I was obliged to fetch the spade, and she stood and watched while I dug, and I dug just where she had lain in the grass, and the grass was shining as if it was dewy, and the water came almost immediately. I had not dug as much as two feet and there was a jet of water as big as a fist, and it spilled over the edges, it was a real spring.

Yes, that's how it's been in the matter of water. It is a good spring, not sweet and not bitter, it does not taste of ice-water or of rock, and I've built a frame round it, like a wall round a well, and I shall finish it this summer, and I shall make a lid. It does not freeze to the bottom in winter so I can answer you like this and tell the County Council that we have water, we have water till our dying day, and we shall leave water behind us, and it is called Theresa's Spring.

# *True Love*

Hällnäs Sanatorium
25th August 1941

Dear Brother

Now I'll sit down to write to you. I have the afternoon before me, you must forgive me if my letter is a long one; you know how unpredictable I am. That your letters are as short as glimpses of the sun in winter I can well understand, you have strong lungs and no fever and so you have neither rest nor peace. You have your fever too in your own way.

My patches and glands have not changed.

Elna and Agda are dead. And Arne away at Bränntjärn – it's a month ago now – he was thought to be getting better, he had had an operation on his ribs and had no doubt that he would be sent home in the autumn. But it flared up, it flared up, and now I must tell you what happened, since I was perhaps not entirely without blame; it flared up and after a week he was gone. He had an easy time of it though he had dreaded it so much. He was thirty-one.

You remember what he was like. Small and fair-haired and easy-going; he played the guitar.

He was keeping company with Vendla, she is only twenty-three and born in Vindelgransele. She is related to the Lindbloms of Ristjöln; she is slender and has a terribly lovely face, she wears her hair in a big bun on her head, she has a strong nose and big lips; she is a believer.

Arne was too. A believer.

Arne and Vendla were fond of going for walks in the forest.

Vendla had two patches on her left lung, but she had got better even since she came here; she says herself that she does not feel a thing, only that perhaps she is a little hotter than usual. Hotter! They are in the habit of going for their walks in the forest after dinner, and usually sit down and rest behind the topmost clump of spruce trees.

And I had seen that, had seen how they sat there twining their fingers together.

And one day towards the end of July – it was a Sunday and hot, burning hot, though I was only wearing a short-sleeved shirt the sweat was pouring from me, as if I'd been in a timber forest – a Sunday it was, when I followed them.

They walked more quickly than I did, and he had his arm round her; she was only wearing a blouse and skirt, and it was a skirt that was as it were slit at the side. I was in no hurry either, one must reserve one's energies and only use those that can give one pleasure. The harebells had come out, and I took an ox-eyed daisy and put it in my shirt pocket.

When I arrived at the topmost point of their forest walk they had already sat down. I could see that Arne was almost annoyed that I had not left them in peace. Vendla moved a comb she had in her hair. She had a bag of chocolates.

But I sat down and we began to talk about the war. I can remember to this day exactly how things were; the spruce gave off the smell of hot sunshine, there were ants in the grass and Arne was wearing a blue silk scarf round his neck under his shirt.

"They'll be taking Russia now," said Arne. "Though what can they want the whole of Siberia for?"

And I said that they probably did not know, they weren't taking Russia in order to use it for anything in particular.

"But if you take something, you can no doubt find some way of using it that gives you pleasure," I said.

"First you help yourself, then you satisfy yourself."

"Hitler is The Beast," said Arne. "He has broken loose and

the whole world looks upon him with amazement. He has got the power to wage war and subdue peoples and all the inhabitants of the world must worship him."

And Vendla said nothing. But I said that it could well be that Hitler was The Beast.

He had read about it in the Book of Revelations at night, he said. He had not been able to sleep. "Fire shall fall from heaven upon the earth and all those who do not worship the Beast shall be killed and peoples shall be led away into captivity, and the Beast is scarlet."

"Hitler's colour is brown," I said.

"But he is scarlet inside," said Arne.

We were half sitting on the grass, a real Sabbath peace reigned; I stretched myself out so that I got a trifle nearer Vendla; you know my long legs and my long stooping back and my hands that I like to have free before me when I talk.

"And he'll soon fall upon us," said Arne. "Sweden will be drowned in blood."

And Vendla, she said nothing, it was as if she was not listening; she had hitched her skirt up a bit over her knees; now and then she helped herself to a chocolate.

"So you think Hitler may concern himself with us. What would he want Sweden for?"

Then he sat silent for a while and thought.

"But surely you can see," he said and pointed to the forest and the hills and the Vindel river.

"Who would not want such a land?" he said.

And it was probably true.

I warned you at the start that I should be writing a long letter. Now you can see.

"But he won't affect us," I said. "What use would a sanatorium be to him?"

And to that Arne had at first nothing to say.

"He will shun us like the plague," I said.

But then Arne said: "We shall be butchered like all the rest."

And then I understood that he was really to be pitied. But what could I do?

"Hitler will butcher us, he won't make any distinction between us," he said.

"You are afraid," I said. "You are really frightened."

"Yes," he said. "I am terribly frightened. And it's worst at night."

And he told me that Vendla had said it was the same for her, though now she sat not saying a word; I'm not even sure that she was listening. She said nothing. You remember that I've always been upset by frightened people. Frightened people, they alarm me.

"Of what should we be afraid?" I said. "We who live on a knife-edge."

"A knife-edge?" he said.

"With this illness," I said. "Our lives can be cut short. At any time. So why should we be afraid?"

"So you mean that if one has consumption one need not fear Hitler?" he said.

That was a difficult question to answer, so I had to think for a while.

"First one accustoms oneself to fear," I tried saying. "You accept it as you accept the taste of a water you have to drink every day. And then you break the habit of calling it fear. And then it is transformed into a sort of hope."

Though that was not really what I meant. I had wanted to say it much better, particularly because Vendla was listening. She had lain down on her back and had a stalk of grass in her mouth.

"So that fear and hope should be as it were the same thing," said Arne, and you could hear that he thought I had got myself into deep waters and he thought he had got the better of me.

"If one is afraid then one just grabs at rescue all the time," I said. "Like a man who is drowning, as if there were nothing but rescue at which one could grab. And one never has time to grab life itself."

And then I said this, which I never should have said: "I celebrate marriage with life each day."

Those were words that Arne couldn't bear to hear, they were too strong for him, they hit home like a blow from a hammer, he began to cough and after that he spoke not a word more to us that day.

But Vendla, she sat up abruptly and looked at me, and it was as if she now really looked at me for the first time. I celebrate marriage with life every day, and small wrinkles appeared round her eyes and she opened her mouth slightly and moved her lips a bit as if she was repeating what I said to herself, and she was incredibly beautiful.

After a while we got up and began to go down the hill. We said nothing more for a long time, and Vendla walked between us, but now she walked a bit nearer to me, a sort of gap seemed to have developed between her and Arne. Arne had suddenly begun to cough a bit, but we walked along kicking stones and bending down to pull up stalks of grass with our fingers and looking up at the clouds and trying to pretend that there was nothing amiss. The heat was closer and more oppressive now, though we were going downhill. And now and then I felt Vendla's hip against mine, it was as if she bumped against me with her buttocks gently and carefully but with determination. I celebrate marriage with life every day, and I could feel how the muscles in her side rolled, and heaved as she walked.

And when we were halfway Vendla said, and I remember it word for word just as she said it: "I am not as frightened as I really might be, not because I am a believer. Not for the sake of eternal life. But because I know that everything is temporary and will pass. Even that in which one believes is only there instead of something else."

And she went on: "You yourself choose what you will believe in and be afraid of and hope for. What one should really believe, that is beyond our reach. Even belief is temporary. So why should one be afraid all the time?" she said.

That is just what she said, word for word.

And when she said that, I felt that she was the wisest human being I had ever met.

Everything is temporary and will pass, and that which is really something in which one should believe, that is beyond reach, therefore people need not be as frightened as they could in fact be.

When we got back to the sanatorium Arne went straight to his room and lay down. He had already understood how things were. His cough got progressively worse, he remained in bed.

That is what has been a torment to me all the time, I should never have said those words, if one lives on a knife-edge you can be infected by a few words: I celebrate marriage with life every day.


That evening I stole into Vendla's room, I got there without anyone seeing me; and she let me in immediately, it was as if she were expecting me.

We hardly talked at all, it was not necessary, for we had already said most of it, but we stood for a long time with our arms round one another, as if we had lived apart for an unbearably long time and at last met again; she rocked backwards and forwards as if one of us needed comforting.

The whole thing was so obvious. And when she undid her bun it seemed to me almost as if she opened her whole self to me, her hair was like the Virgin Mary's veil in a painting. Her room faces west so that she had the sunlight over her; and we were both so excited that we became breathless and were slightly aware of our coughs; true love is short and flickering.

But for Arne things went quickly. During the next few days he had several minor haemorrhages and did not leave his room any more. We were not told anything, Vendla and I, here one is never told anything.

Vendla has a sister in Avaträsk, they are said to be so alike that one cannot tell one from the other. She runs the café there and belongs to the choir in the mission house. You can go there and see her. Then you will know.

But on the last day of Arne's life I was allowed in to see him; one is not usually allowed. There wasn't much left of him, you know how it is. And he wanted me to read to him.

It was the First Epistle of John. "Herein is our love made perfect, that we may have boldness in the day of judgement because as He is, so are we in this world. There is no fear in love; but perfect love casteth out fear; because fear hath torment. He that feareth is not made perfect in love." And later that night he died.

I have wanted to tell you about this; you knew Arne in Bränntjärn, and sometimes I feel I have some sort of responsibility for things going as they did; I should never have said what I did about what I do with life every day.

But it is most probable that he had had a cavity for a long time.

I must end now, it is supper time and I want to send this off at once, I don't want this to lie about, that haunting anxiety will never leave me and Vendla. She is waiting for me up in the hall.

I hope that life is strong and good for you each day, and that you will hold out.

Greetings to everyone.

Your loving brother.

# The Stump-Grubber

It is an implement.

I tell you this so that you may understand that it is not a human being nor a monster, neither is it only wood, and bits of iron and cable and hook.

Three large sturdy legs made of wooden posts and on top the pulley, and then the cog-wheels, it is the cog-wheels and the pulley that do all the work, and on its side a winch of iron, and you put the cable round what is to be lifted, a stone or a stump, and you fasten the cable with the hook, and then you wind the winch round, and for each turn you make with the winch you lift the stone or the stump a fraction of an inch, your strength is multiplied a thousandfold. With a stump-grubber a poor weak creature can raise slaughtered horses and stones that are fast in the ground.

He needs help, though, to carry the stump-grubber and put it in place.

But if you lose your grip and if you have not locked the winch with the ratchet, then the object you have lifted falls back and all the power returns to the winch and that power is converted into speed and it whirls round so quickly that you cannot see it, and it crushes without mercy everything that comes in its way. Then the winch is like the hand of God's wrath.

Jacob Lundmark and Gerda, Jacob's Gerda, they lived on the smallholding in Inreliden. They had bought the partition in 1918. He had himself sawn the wood for the house and built it, and he had cleared and cultivated two fields so that they fed a cow; in the winter he was out in the timber-forest, and in summer he hewed charcoal-wood for the farmers. He had built the cowshed out of old timber that he had bought from Eric Markström in Bök. He was not a big stout man, Jacob, but tough and muscular; his nose had been crooked since his childhood, he had been kicked while helping to shoe a horse.

That was when he was ten, his job was to hold up the back legs, he stood just behind the horse. Then his mother, Alfrida, came out and saw him standing there – he was the apple of her eye – and she shouted to the men: "No, Jacob mustn't lift the hooves, it's dangerous."

And he abruptly straightened up to say that he was indeed not too small to give the blacksmith a hand, and the horse didn't like that and ever since then his nose had been crooked and he had a red mark just under his right eye.

Gerda, she was from Örträsk, so she didn't know anyone and no one knew anything about her for certain, so she was on her own. The only person she talked to occasionally was Isabella, Isabella Stenlund, the woman who had the illegitimate son. But that was only a few times a year. On the wall she had a hanging, it was one of the corduroy hangings, a blue one, and it said on it:

THE MYSTERY OF FAITH
IN A PURE CONSCIENCE

It was probably taken from the first Epistle of Timothy. She was plump but not fat.

Between the house and the cowshed at Inreliden Jacob had left a pine-tree, a huge pine which he thought could be a kind of good-luck tree; he had spared it. No one could embrace it though many had tried, not even Nylundius the preacher, though he could embrace seven feet; and the forester Nicolin had said that it might well be the largest pine in the Norsjö, and even in the area of Lycksele he did not know of a bigger one.

But Gerda was of the opinion that the big pine was as it were gloomy and depressing and that it kept out the light; she liked light, she delighted in it, so at last Jacob took it down and had it sawn up, and out of it he made a bed, a big wide bed, and a gate-legged table and six folding chairs, and a door for the small room – before they'd only had a piece of drapery there. That was in 1924, and their third girl Dagny, she was two years old.

But the stump was left.

And even the stump was enormous. A district forester came all the way from Ruskträsk just to see it, and to measure it and count its rings, and he said that the big pine had been like Methuselah, its days were like those of the sand.

And Jacob said that that stump was too much for him, its roots went out into the Vindel river to the south and out into the Skellefte river in the north, the big pine had certainly drunk from two rivers at the same time.

But to Gerda the stump was hateful, a human being sees what he has an eye for. It was in the way, she wanted to plant currant bushes there, or they could put in raspberries. Isabella could give them the plants, it was somehow a savage and ungodly thing on their farm where she wanted everything to be smooth and neat; it was a graven image.

So she said: "Dearest love, Jacob, can't you get rid of that stump?"

"I don't know whether I'm equal to it," said Jacob.

"You can burn it up, or bury it, or prize it loose with a crow-bar. It makes me feel ill, it is hateful and nasty."

"A stump like that has superhuman strength," said Jacob. "An ordinary human being was never meant to fight with a primitive monster like that."

But in the summer Jacob got hold of a ghastly stump-grubber, it was up for sale at the auction of the effects of Elis of Lillåberg; the legs were twenty feet long, it was the stump-grubber they had had when they made the Ajaur road. He got it cheap, it was a sort of monstrosity and a show-off, almost impossible to use – big men like Elis of Lillåberg don't exist these days. Jacob got it home on an open-sided wagon, as he had already borrowed Gabriel Israelsson's horse and was going in the direction of Svartlidlen.

By the last Saturday in July he had got in the hay and then he set the stump-grubber beside the stump of the great pine.

And he thought: "Men walk upon the earth like trees. And those who serve not He will tear out by their roots."

He exposed the thickest roots with a spade and with his axe he chopped off everything that he could get at for the moment, and then he dug deeper and took his pick-axe and even an iron bar; and he chopped and prized loose so that he could remove the small stones and moraine soil with his fingers; when the bark was cracked a smell of turpentine came from the stump; the earth smelt too; and he hewed off the tough roots with his axe, and it didn't worry him that it struck sparks out of the gravel and became blunt; it was for Gerda's sake he was doing this, and once he had started upon the stump there was no question of turning back and no mercy, he couldn't worry over the bluntness of his big axe, he could grind it on Monday.

He was dripping with sweat and he had to take off his blue smock, but he always sweated horribly when he became eager and was putting his back into it, and the gravel tore his cuticles and his knuckles so that they bled, but he took no notice; the roots were as thick as the thigh-bone of a horse and were just as many as the boughs had been on the pine itself while it was still alive; and when he stuck his crow-bar down into the ground he continually struck new roots that went in all directions in the depths; and he began to imagine that it was the pine that had held together his whole plot with its roots, and that if he were finally able to lift the stump the whole of Inreliden would crash together and be scattered; and when he dug and heaved and lifted the roots with his crow-bar, then he was aware that there was still life in that stump, the roots bent a trifle but only enough to make their strength and toughness apparent; and he said to that stump that, true enough, you are terrific, but a man too is tough and he has

114

muscles and he can work out one thing and another that are beyond your powers of understanding, and moreover he has his stump-grubber.

At last he was forced to straighten up and go in to Gerda and drink some water.

"Aren't you going to take a rest soon?" she said. "It is Saturday after all."

"I'm only working on that stump," he said, "only by way of passing the time."

Then he went out and carried on.

When the time came for them to eat their evening porridge she came out and called him; he only ate one plate of barley-meal porridge. And she asked if she should not wash the small wounds on his knuckles and if he would not pull off his dirty clothes and put on his new trousers and his light-coloured shirt. It was after all the weekend, and the children wanted them to sing together and to read stories from the fairy-tale book.

But he heard from her voice that she had only one thing in her mind, that was the stump.

"It isn't really any sort of work," he said. "This job with the stump, I'm only trying to feel my way, and to reckon how I can best get it out."

He looked at her, her downy arms, her round chin, the little dimples in her cheeks, the grey-blue eyes that were sorrowful and happy at the same time – they were like some sort of warm spring – and on her forehead the little wrinkle that the parson had said meant deep thoughts.

And he suddenly felt almost happy to think that he might still be lucky enough to raise the stump and that when morning came she would be able to come out and view the big hole in the ground.

The earth was harder and harder the deeper he dug; the pebbles and gravel and clay were packed together so that they were almost like boulders, and he couldn't understand how the roots had penetrated them down in the depths, they might even have eaten their way into the rock; it was as if the pine had decided to stand for ever and ever.

But at last the largest roots were dug loose and chopped off and free.

Then he fetched the stump-grubber. He lifted first one leg then another, only a few feet at a time: if he hurried, the stump-grubber might get the upper hand and crash down – besides he had the whole night. He stood aside a few paces to see whether he had got it into the right position, and when he saw that the cog-wheel and pulley were right over the stump, he stamped it fast into the ground with his feet and his iron post.

Then he took the steel cable and pushed it in under the stump, under the roots that he could get at, and pulled it up in several places, under the worst of the thick roots, and finally fastened it firmly in place with the hook, the big iron hook, so that there could be no mistake, nothing could come loose, and the weight would be evenly balanced so that nothing could go wrong; now it was as it were an even contest between him and the stump.

And he sat down there on the grass and looked at the cable and the pulley and the winch, and the stump-grubber. And the stump.

"Now," he thought. "Now."

And he thought: "Gerda is standing behind the curtain watching me."

And he asked himself this too: "What is she thinking?" He had never been certain of what she was thinking – though no human being knows what love or hatred in others he has to deal with.

What were they thinking down in Örträsk?

First he wound the winch the number of turns needed to tense the cable, then he stopped to see that it had not gone slack under some root – it is important that the steel cable should always be stretched, that it is straight and that there is not any dislocation or weakness in it – then he made a few more turns so that the cable began to sing, it sounded as the ice on a lake does when it is going to break up.

When you use a stump-grubber you must not be in a hurry, you must stop from time to time, there is a ratchet that you can drop down against the cog-wheels to which the winch is fastened so that it does not unwind.

Then he made one turn at a time and rested a bit between each turn, it wasn't possible to make more than one turn at a time.

The half turn when the winch is going up is done with the muscles of a man's arms, back and legs; when the winch goes the half turn down, you lean on it with the upper part of your body and press it down with your weight.

In a little while the small roots began to give way, you could hear a snap far down in the earth when they broke, and Jacob thought: "All the same it is moving, it is not invincible."

That means half a turn at a time; and when the winch is going down one can lean against it and rest for a few breaths.

And he thought: "If it were not for the fact that this undertaking is mine, if this hadn't been put solely and only on me, then I would have spoken to Gerda and asked her to come out and help me, by leaning on the winch with the little bit of weight that she has after all."

It was the south side of the stump that gave way first, it snapped so much that at first he thought it was the cable that was being torn apart, but then when he got the winch down he saw that the stump had risen some half inch and that the earth had cracked round the roots where he had not dug and he said: "Dear God, let it give way on the north side too."

But he didn't want to let down the ratchet on the wheel yet, the ratchet of a stump-grubber ticks like a clock; if you use the ratchet you can't lift anything silently.

After yet a few more turns only the south side was moving: "I shall have to fasten it firm with the ratchet," he thought, "and dig and chop a bit on the north side, otherwise it will tilt over. And then I shall have to let it down once more and start again from the beginning. I'll do three turns more," he thought. "Only three turns. No more."

                    *       *       *

Now he had to exert himself to the full. And he could feel how the
veins on the outside of his neck were swelling so that they pressed
against the neck-band of his sweater, and what a strain it was on
his thighs and arms so that it was almost like having cramp, and
the red mark under his right eye throbbed, and the winch cut into
his palms so they were on the way to being flayed. "Perhaps I
ought to let down the ratchet, take a rest and put on my gloves,"
he thought.

Never before in his life had he exerted himself in this way. But
neither was this work in the ordinary meaning of the word. It
wasn't only that he had said: "I shall go at it and get up that stump
before I take a rest day, that huge stump." No, he had a quite
special sort of obligation and there was no mercy, and there
behind the curtain in the living room Gerda was watching him.

"For the sake of that a man can give up everything," he
thought. "For the sake of that a man can forget himself so that he
is no longer aware of the blood and sinews of his own body."

And confirmation: there came a snap like a gun-shot on the
north side and the whole stump shook like an animal wearing a
slaughtering-mask and the south side sank down a fraction so that
the north side should have room to rise.

"Gerda," thought Jacob. "Gerda."

"Now I'll take no more rests," he thought, "now I'll not drop
the ratchet, now it's a matter of not giving up, now I have the
better of it and I won't let it go, even if I have to fight until the
morning."

The only question was: would the steel cable hold?

After each turn that he now took roots rose a half inch or so,
they split there in the earth and cracked and groaned and broke as
if they'd been strands of wool, and the little stones and the earth
ran back into the hole, and the little roots that had not broken
came up and were peeled; it almost felt as if the stump was giving
up and blessed him. And he hardly took a rest when each turn was
completed, if he had stopped the pain and ache in his hand might

get the better of him; and he thought that no human being had ever pulled such a mighty stump out of the ground, there was almost something solemn about it, and Gerda is standing there and sees how calmly and firmly I wind the winch of the stump-grubber.

And very soon the stump hung almost free, it rocked and swayed a trifle on the cable and sometimes it tilted as if in its helplessness it were trying to shake itself loose; it was even larger and more horrible than Jacob had thought, you could clearly see that it was by nature infernal, it was as it were shaggy.

And the cable sang like the strings of a violin.

If he could only get it up high enough to be able to lift it to one side with a pole and lay it down on the edge of the hole then everything would be over, then he'd take a rest, then he would go in to Gerda and say: "I pulled up that stump, I got him up because I had the stump-grubber there."

At last there were only two roots holding the stump to the earth, they were half peeled and as stretched and tormented as the sinews of Jacob's body, they trembled as if they'd been alive. They were on the north side.

Jacob thought about his hands, he'd lost all feeling in them; "they are benumbed, they are benumbed by pain," he thought, "perhaps the skin will fall off them like a pair of gloves; after this is over, and after I've had a rest, then I'll let my hands rest too, then I'll submerge them in cold water, and let them take a holiday and get back their strength, for one's hands are the body's crown."

And just then, just when it was all nearly over, Gerda came out on to the porch – he did not see her as he was standing at the back of the stump – and she was holding Dagny by one hand and in the other she had Dagny's doll, and she called with all the strength she had in her body.

"Dearest love Jacob! You must be careful!"

And that call, that was the most wonderful thing Jacob had been sensible of in the whole of his life, it was so inexpressibly warm and trembling, and so permeated with concern and love that he halted half way through the winch, her call had made him quite weak and dazed, he felt that he must see her, and he turned his head and the upper part of his body so that she would perhaps be in sight, but he still held on to the winch, and he could really see her, she was standing in the porch and in her left hand she held the little girl and in her right hand the doll, and the evening sun lit her up from the side so that he could see how her apron clung to her stomach and thighs, and she had bound up her hair with a blue shawl, and her mouth was open, and her eyes were wide open with anxiety and fondness. No human being could seem more heavenly.

And she called to him once more: "Dearest love – Jacob, you must be careful!"

And just as she called for the second time, he got the feeling back in his hands, and he could feel that they couldn't do any more; his fingers began to straighten themselves out and he could not stop them, it felt as if there was no longer any mercy for them, and he tried to make the half turn that was wanting to bring the winch down to the bottom, but he had not the strength.

And then the last rootlets broke, they gave way suddenly and the stump, which was now hanging free, tipped over and swung round as if it were possessed by a frightful fit of rage, and Jacob was quite helpless, all he could hear was Gerda's voice within him, and the thickest root of the stump gave him a horrible blow on his hip-joint, just on the sinews of his hip, a tremendous blow on his hip so that he fell forwards and his fingers gave way altogether, and all the strength in the stump went back into the winch. But within him all he saw was Gerda, and he was bursting with her voice and her words, the eagerness and anxiety and warmth, her fondness for him that was so great that there were almost tears in her voice, so that when he fell headlong he did not grasp what it was that was happening, he did not realize what had befallen him. What it was that struck him like the hand of God's wrath and tore his breast open and killed him, if it was the winch, or if it was the almost unbearable heat of love, there are words that are like glowing coals, dearest love Jacob, you must be careful.

# Boundaries

There were four farms in Korpmyrberget, Enar's, Anton's, Oscar's and Otto's. Otto's was in the middle, it was surrounded by the other three.

Each farm consisted of 4.942 acres, and along the boundaries square stones had been placed.

Enar and Anton and Oscar were married and had heaps of children; Otto was unmarried and childless; he was thickset and his face was as wrinkled as a workman's glove.

The farm was the only thing close to his heart; he knew his farm as he did his own body – it was dry and barren.

If he had any joy in life it was in his farm, Korpmyrberget 1:1.

So it was not surprising that he should want his farm to grow and be developed; that is what we want to happen with those we love.

He began to move the boundary stones, he did it carefully and in secret, and at night, just a few feet; he carried them across his thighs, with bent knees and unsteadily.

"If I do it carefully," he thought, "then Enar and Anton and Oscar will never notice anything, no one can remember so precisely where the boundaries run, not within a few inches; the earth and universe are remoulded continuously but so slowly and protractedly that we are not aware of it. Bays get clogged with weeds, streams alter their course, trees fall and rot, mountains sink and the deeps rise up."

But at last Enar and Anton and Oscar became suspicious. A heap of stones that Enar had always believed was his suddenly became Otto's. And Anton's path that led down to Korpmyrtarn now ran through Otto's forest. And a couple of huge pine trees that Oscar had rejoiced in ever since his childhood had wandered off and one day stood on Otto's ground.

So they consulted among themselves.

But if it were not Otto but someone else?

And if one had known for certain where the boundaries really ran.

If only Otto were the sort you could talk to.

And if it had been a matter of life and death.

So they agreed to wait and see; it might be that Otto was suffering from an illness, this moving of the boundary stones, a sort of impulse.

But when four years had passed Otto began to take their arable land.

Then they wrote a letter to the Land Surveyor's Board in Umeå: the boundaries of Korpmyrberget 1:1 must be redrawn or staked out anew.

So one day in September the surveyor came; it was to Otto that he came. In a leather bag he had a surveyor's chain and a theodolite and pencils and a ruler and other instruments. He was a calm, quiet surveyor, he wore balloon-breeches and puttees and his hair was parted with a ruler.

He said that two executives from the Land Surveyor's Office would have to be called, but Otto said there was no hurry, first of all the surveyor must have a bite to eat.

So Otto made barley-meal porridge and put out milk and cranberries, and then he sat down on the wood-box and regarded the surveyor. He ate slowly; he did not seem to be eating because he was hungry, but because it was his duty. He kept his left hand spread out and dead still on the table-top and he sat straight and still on his chair; he looked like a seven-inch nail, and he did not bend forwards when he ate, yet all the same he never spilt anything, and he ate in squares, he made straight edges with his spoon, he had put the porridge in the middle of the plate and he smoothed it and made the corners quite rectangular, and then he ate carefully and exactly as much from each side so that the porridge was all the time a perfect square; even the last spoonful of barley-meal porridge was square.

"You eat in squares," said Otto, "I've never seen that before."

"If you ever for a moment allow disorder into your life," said the surveyor, "then you are lost."

"Are you always so precise with everything you do?" said Otto.

"I am a man with backbone," said the surveyor; "so far I have never taken a step or performed a manipulation by chance."

"It is of course very fortunate," said Otto, "never to be dependent on chance."

"If you give chance a little finger, she will immediately take your whole hand," said the surveyor. "If you take chance in your boat, you will then have to row her to land."

"So you plan to be precise about this business in Korpmyrberget?" said Otto.

"I shall do everything anew," said the surveyor. "I shall stake out every boundary as it was from the beginning."

"You certainly seem to know the meaning of your life," said Otto.

"Life is entirely meaningless," said the surveyor. "That is why order is so indispensable."

"I believe," said Otto, "that life has a meaning."

"If life itself had a meaning," said the surveyor, "then no laws or boundaries would be needed."

Then Otto realized that the surveyor was an impossible person. He wanted to bring to an end all those small improvements to the boundaries of his property which it had cost so much toil and so many years to bring about; he was without compassion or mercy. To him one farm was just as sacred as the next.

So that when they got outside Otto went to his wood-shed, fetched his axe and killed him. He was obliged to, the surveyor had just opened that enormous bag. Otto killed him in secret, and then carried him to the dung-pit. Getting rid of a surveyor is not all that simple, he buried him a good three feet down.

He carried the bag up to the attic for you never know – that chain was brass and the bag was ox-hide, real shoe-leather.

For a time there was of course talk about that surveyor who had disappeared. No one had seen him. They formed a human chain in Björksele and dragged half way to Korpmyrberget, and the constable went round for a time to the farms and asked if anyone had seen a townsman in balloon-breeches, but later on they said that he must certainly have drowned in the Vindel river. Otto did not know anything, he hadn't even been expecting a surveyor. It might also be the case that that surveyor had lost his way and would eventually appear on Ammarnäs or Sorsele.

Soon people had forgotten him.

Anton and Enar and Oscar went to Sikseleberg and stayed there over the winter working the timber forest, and they never once remembered to talk about the surveying of the land.

When spring came Otto moved the muck, he took the largest part of the dung-pit to the potato-field. He used a bushel; he spread the dung with a pitchfork, and when he prodded the heap with the pitchfork there was nothing that was solid and had not decayed.

The wonderful thing about a dung-pit is the way in which it ferments and burns and refines. It is like a charcoal stack where everything is changed, but nothing is finally lost.

After that he had to set his potatoes.

No, there was nothing left of the surveyor, not even his boots or puttees or balloon-breeches, nor yet his skeleton, including that backbone he had talked of, it was all gone. And Otto was almost pleased that the surveyor in this case had been so obliging and compliant and had disappeared so amicably and meekly. Though when he was nearly at the bottom of the muck-pit the cranium got stuck on one of the prongs of the pitchfork.

The acids and the fermentation and the warmth had not bitten into it one bit; it may have been that the surveyor's head had been firmer and more immovable and he had denser material in his skull than elsewhere. And Otto put it to one side: it was a large, impressive skull, it would be negligent and wasteful just to throw it away – it is a great sin to let any created thing be destroyed.

Otto always wanted to do his best.

When he had nearly finished setting the potatoes, when he was in the middle of the last row, he went and fetched the skull and put a large potato with many eyes in it just behind the frontal bone. He then put the cranium and the potato in the sunniest row, which was usually the most productive.

That summer he again allowed himself to move a dozen boundary stones: he and his farm mustn't become rigid from anxiety or placidity.

He lifted the potatoes at the end of September. He knelt in order to spare his back.

He had forgotten that he had put one potato in a skull.

Therefore he was in a way astonished when he dug it up.

It was on the second day of the potato lifting, about mid-day, the potato had bred most supernaturally, the cranium was full of new potatoes, as if a field-mouse had made its hiding place in it. The potatoes lay in curved carefully arranged rows, like logs in a stack or piglets when they are sucking, as the thoughts must once have lain in the surveyor's head.

And Otto knocked the potatoes out of the skull into his cloth cap and carried them in and put them in the larder. The skull was left to dry for a time, then he pounded it into meal, one can't lightly allow growing power like that to be wasted.

Then in the autumn he made two cow necklaces of the surveyor's chain, they looked like necklaces of pure gold.

When he had killed the pig and was going to eat the ears and the tail and the trotters he took out his surveyor potatoes.

After half an hour they were still not cooked.

When he tested them with a fork after an hour it still could not penetrate the peel.

Boiling only seemed to make them harder, the fork rang when after two hours he had another try. Towards evening the water had boiled away, the potatoes lay rattling in the bottom of the pan.

The surveyor potatoes had turned into stones. Square stones. They looked like boundary stones.

He put them back in the larder.

And he got himself a maid who declared that she really could boil potatoes. Boiling potatoes is the foundation of all human life.

And she boiled them for fourteen days, the fourteen days she was with him, they seemed to become sort of shiny outside.

He never touched the girl; he did not even bother to look at her though she undressed in the kitchen in the evenings and stood there just in her underwear.

And in May he set the potatoes again, even the surveyor potatoes. You never can know anything for certain.

During the summer, stones increased on the potato field, they came up everywhere, a tip and a side here, a flat surface there. They looked like boundary stones.

So he began to pick up and carry. He made a little sledge on two shafts, a sledge with a birch-bark basket to use for picking up stones. He put the stones on the mound of stones below the wood-shed.

In August he built a supporting wall by the shed wall, it was easily done with those square stones; the mound was soon up to the eaves.

The skin of his hands was worn, his back was injured by stone-picking, he had horrid pains in his hips and shoulders.

His sleep was affected, it is a disgrace for a man to have stonier land than others.

In September he tried to lift the potatoes. The few he found among the stones were no bigger than a thumbnail, and gave no more than half a barrel. The boundary stones had quite got the upper hand, those square stones that had been created in the surveyor's skull, just behind the frontal bone.

He was obliged to build a new mound behind the flax-drying shed. At night he took the stable lantern, dipped the light and hung it round his neck by a strap, so that he could see to scrape and pluck up and garner his unnatural harvest.

He tormented himself to such a degree that the blood forced its way up to his mouth. But he never tried to boil a single stone; in fact he never gave himself time to cook any proper food. He ate swedes and turnips raw and hacked pieces off the dried fish.

And the potato field sank and dropped below the surrounding land; the stones that he had moved had eaten and drunk the top soil.

On All Saints' Day he gave up. He gave up and lay quite still for two days on the kitchen sofa. The wall clock never struck for he had given up winding it. He covered his face with two loose pages from the collection of sermons: the First Death and the Judgement.

On the third day he made his way to Malå and went to see the doctor, Doctor Rudvall.

And Otto told him about his back and his hands and his hips and knees and feet. Yes, he gave an account of the whole of his body.

"So could I get a pain-killer?" he said.

The doctor examined him.

It was all very simple, a blind man could have seen it: his back was finished, his hands were worn out and his hips were crooked and his knees destroyed by pain and his feet done for.

Then the doctor asked how so much misery and deficiency had accumulated in one body.

Then Otto told him how things were, his potato field was infested by stones and he had to rip out this infestation by the roots. Square stones grew like weeds out of the soil, little boundary stones reproduced themselves quite recklessly.

And Dr Rudvall realized that it was the stones and the potato field that were the illness.

In the evening they went together to Korpmyrberget; it was night by the time they got there. Otto's whole body was in pieces and he wanted to go to bed, but the doctor simply had to see these stones that belonged to the vegetable kingdom.

So Otto fetched the lantern – there was a hoar-frost – and he bent down and picked up a surveyor stone and shone a light on it.

And the doctor stood for a long time and peered, and he twisted his head this way and that as if he wanted to view the stone from all sides.

Then he said: "I can't see anything."

"Don't you see the stone?" said Otto.

"No," said the doctor, "I can't see the stone."

Then Otto lifted the lantern still nearer, he held it an inch from his hand and said: "But, don't you see?"

But Dr Rudvall said: "No. I can only see your empty hand."

Then Otto held his hand in front of his eyes, and suddenly even he saw that the palm was empty.

"I must have dropped the stone," he said.

And he picked up another stone, he took hold of it with all his five fingers and gripped it as hard as he could and held it out to the doctor.

"What about this?" he said.

But again the doctor said: "No, I can't for the life of me see any stone."

And then Otto could feel that his fingers were squeezing empty air and themselves as if they were affected by cramp, and he said: "It's my hands. They won't do their work as they should."

And he gave the lantern to the doctor and went down on his knees and dug with both hands into the earth; and he saw surveyor stones everywhere, but no sooner did he try to take hold of them than they disappeared, they crumbled to bits and turned into nothing but earth, they were elusive. He crawled here and there over the upper corner of the potato field, he struggled and groped and fumbled and the hoar-frost burnt his palms like fire, but he could not capture a single stone. At last he had to stand up and look at the doctor, who stood holding the stable lantern in front of him. It was plain to see that he understood the whole matter: Otto felt as if the doctor saw right through him, nothing could be hidden from Doctor Rudvall, and boundary stones that seem to multiply uncontrollably in a potato field, such a thing never happens to a person by chance.

"I shall never understand life," said Otto.

"Yes," said the doctor. "It is a sort of mystery. Life."

"Can you wait a moment?" said Otto. "I only want to fetch an implement."

So he went to the wood-shed – he had no choice – and he fetched his axe that was stuck fast in the wall, then he went back to the doctor and killed him, he killed him secretly and then he dragged him by the feet to his dung-pit and buried him. Thereupon he went indoors and went to bed. His whole body was aching so much that he was only half conscious. He fell asleep immediately and slept for forty-eight hours, in spite of the fact that he had not been given a pain-killer.

The search for Dr Rudvall was frenzied, the people of Malå went round Får swamp and Malå swamp to see whether he had floated to the surface; patients sat from morning to night in case by chance . . . ; the constable went between the villages and single farms asking after him; the river Mal was dragged as far down as Strömfors. The like of Dr Rudvall they would never be able to get, at least not in Malå – he had been quite like a normal human being, like God's chosen man.

But then on a Sunday came the snow, three feet in six days, and after that it was no use worrying any more about Dr Rudvall.

Otto was in a poor way all winter. He looked after his animals, carried in wood and lit the stove, and that was all he did – no carpentry, nothing in the smithy. It was the first winter that he was without occupation, he who was otherwise so wonderfully clever with his hands.

But the day after Holy Thursday he carted out the dung.

Nothing was left of Dr Rudvall, his clothes were gone, and his false teeth and his beard and his cranium, he was gone for ever. Otto didn't even have him in mind as he scooped out the muck. All the same it was God's blessing that he was so far recovered that he could handle the pitchfork.

But then he got up the hand, it was the doctor's right hand, it was quite fresh and undamaged, it was so steeped and saturated with medicine that it could not possibly decay; the forefinger was outstretched as if there was something that should be pointed out.

When later on Otto set the potatoes he took the doctor's hand and put a potato into it, a fine large kidney potato, and he closed the fingers round it – it would be a shame not to use such an excellent hand – and he set it in the lowest row but one.

It was a summer with night rain and great warmth, a real potato summer.

Otto lifted the potatoes in the last week of September, the frost had already melted down the tops; he had wrapped some sacking round his trouser legs so that he could kneel and dig.

In the last row but one he found the doctor's hand again.

Of the hand itself very little was left, and of the large potato the hand had grasped, nothing but a slimy smear, but round about it were the loveliest new potatoes.

They were large potatoes, yellow, uniform, smooth-skinned kidneys, and each was as it were five, they looked like a bony hand with five fingers, even the joints and the nails were visible, this is how the five-finger kidney potatoes arose, they were the most beautiful potatoes Otto had seen in the whole of his life.

There are said to be five-finger kidney potatoes in Storselbränna even today, you can get seed potatoes of them there. Otto is said to have given half a bucketful to a cousin who lived there.

Otto tried eating one that evening and the potato was like yolk of egg, and this single potato was nearly a whole meal; the rest he put aside for seed-potatoes. They were possibly a trifle difficult to peel round the joints.

After two years Otto only had one row of ordinary kidney potatoes, the rest were five-fingered ones.

And he got better and more active, his back and his feet healed, and his hips straightened themselves out and his hands and knees recovered, now and then he felt strong enough to move some of the boundary-stones towards Enar, Anton and Oscar; there seemed to be something healing and health-giving about those five-fingered kidney potatoes.

And the surveyor stones were largely gone from the potato field.

When Dr Rudvall had been gone for three years his nurse married Constable Hultin in Malå, she had given up hope.

That autumn she heard of a man in Lycksele direction who made keyhole mountings that were supernaturally beautiful and well made.

It was Otto who made these keyhole mountings, he made them out of the surveyor's bag that he had put away in the attic.

The nurse and Constable Hultin came to see him on the last Sunday in September; they had left the horse and trap in Startliden and walked the last mile; and Otto got out the keyhole mountings.

And the nurse asked him how he had managed. She had never before seen such lovely curlicues and delicate curves; no, she had not even been able to imagine them. Otto was truly a divinely inspired artist, his keyhole mountings were as it were saturated with beauty and spirituality.

Then Otto produced the punches and pressing forms that he had forged and carved; he grew strangely warm inside when he listened to her; he even brought the press that he had built for the keyhole mountings, it was a gigantic screw-clamp with three thick wooden screws.

Even Constable Hultin thought it was an admirable and wonderful piece of apparatus, and Otto became so excited that he brought out a bit of leather to show how he made those mountings. It hardly ever happened that people talked to him, he actually sweated with eagerness and joy, and while they were standing there talking, she caught sight of a bucket of potatoes that stood half under the table, and she said: "Those are remarkable potatoes."

"They are five-fingered kidney potatoes," said Otto. "I cultivated that sort in a hand I had got hold of," he explained.

Then the nurse picked up a potato and looked at it; she looked especially carefully at what might be called the potato's forefinger.

And quite suddenly she remembered something she had ordered herself to forget.

She had always wanted Dr Rudvall for her own, and one day in the May of the last year – he was in Malå – she had told him so; she could not do without him, he could do what he liked with her, for her he was the meaning of life, she wanted to belong to him for ever.

All he had said was that he was not made in such a way that he wanted her.

That might have meant anything. That evening she bit his forefinger. A man had come from Mörtjärn who had chopped his leg to pieces with an axe, and when the doctor had sewn up his wound, and she had to bite off the thread, she was overcome by a horrid impulse and set her teeth into Dr Rudvall's forefinger and bit him so hard that afterwards she had to help him to sew it up.

And he of course had a deep scar.

It was this scar that she now saw on Otto's five-fingered kidney potatoes. She picked up several potatoes and examined them, and on every one there was this scar.

"It is a curious thing about the human bite," she said; "it is so hot that it is reproduced throughout creation like the glow through a lump of peat."

And she asked: "In whose hand was it that the parent potato grew?"

And Otto the cultivator, the creator, swelled with pride. "It was Dr Rudvall's," he said.

Constable Hultin saw immediately what this meant.

Before they set off – now of course they all three went together – she bought six keyhole mountings from Otto.

Otto made a cone of the First Death and then of the Judgement, and put in them twelve five-fingered kidney potatoes, the new sort which were probably the great symbol and meaning in his life.

"You can even eat them raw," he said. "As picnic food."

"Our whole life," he added, "our whole life is one single uninterrupted wonder."

In time one of his sister's sons took over the farm; at night time he is in the habit of moving one or other of the boundary stones towards Anton, Enar and Oscar.

And they let him be, he only moves them a foot at a time; to set about him would be meaningless: he is that sort of person and he can't control himself. In his heart of hearts he is pure and blameless; he is innocent of his impulses; no man creates his own impulses. He is not going to give up until he has moved the last boundary stone to the ends of the earth.

# The Weight-Lifter

One day in May at Åhlen's in Klaraberg Street the Spirit came upon Anette Svensson.

She had bought sausage, carrots, milk and hard-bread. The Spirit came upon her just after she had paid and was swinging the plastic basket containing her goods up off the steel-topped counter in front of the cashier.

Anette Svensson was twenty-one and she lived alone. Earlier on she had tried, as an experiment, living with three different men. She believed it had become clear to her that love was a mystery. It was raining.

Came upon her is what it did – that's what she thought. She also thought, struck, possessed, penetrated, filled to the brim.

And, in passing, "laughing gas", she thought.

It is true she had never had laughing gas. She only knew it by name, but all the same. The Spirit is a kind of laughing gas.

She had never belonged to any religious sect, she had not even been confirmed. All this came out bit by bit in the police investigation.

Her outlook on life was sometimes dark, sometimes sunny. She lacked an outlook on life.

She did not see the rain and she did not feel it against the skin of her face. She went down the steps to Vasa Street; perhaps the drops in the air about her evaporated because of the heat she had suddenly begun to radiate.

Later on she herself would say that she felt herself filled by a hidden strength; that her feet moved perplexedly and without effort; that she had lost her foothold but neither did she need it;

that she had voluntarily, yes ultra-voluntarily, delivered herself over to the afore-mentioned strength; that she had all at once seen through a secret the nature of which she did not understand; that with absolute certainty she knew something that was unknown, unknown to her; that two play-school classes on the way to Drottning Street were lit up by a dazzling but invisible sun.

The rain, of which Anette Svensson was not aware, had made the asphalt slippery, and in Vasa Street twenty metres ahead of her, a pedestrian, an actor from Västerås, was, at that very moment, run over by a taxi-cab.

Just when the accident happened, just when she heard the dull thud and the screeching tyres and the onlookers' frightened yell, just at that very second she had thought: "Why must the Spirit also descend upon the innocent?"

The actor was crushed tight under the front wheels of the cab; he lay quite still, like a mechanic who had fallen asleep at his work; he kept his mouth half open as if he were searching for a line. A considerable crowd had quickly gathered round him; Anette Svensson heard voices calling out: "He's not breathing! The back of his head is crushed! He is dead! His spine is broken! His chest has been squashed in!"

She particularly noticed a group of women; the taxi-driver, who was sitting in his cab frightened and unhappy, was also staring intently at these women. They were holding their hands to their mouths to check their screams; they were all enormously fat – there were only five of them but with their huge bodies they took up as much space as twenty ordinary people. In their midst stood a tall and very thin man with a sad haggard face and a drooping moustache.

No one made a move to intervene or to fetch help, everyone seemed to regard it as something completed and final. On many faces there shone a look of unusual peace, as if this situation had been the soothing and satisfying goal of a quest that had been going on for a long time, a quest for exactly what was precisely complete and final.

This immorality frightened Anette Svensson: it seemed to her more horrible than the accident itself. And the Spirit in the form of an inner voice said to her: "Get going, Anette Svensson, all release begins with movement!"

Here the writer must temporarily make himself heard above the text. "Can a person really hear inner voices? Are not the occurrences of inner voices signs of illness and decay, presaging the dissolution and splitting of the personality, a threat to, why even a cancellation of the existing compact between the self and the world? Should not the healthy man's innermost being be full of silence?"

"Yes," says the writer.

"No," says the text. "Inner voices are quite normal occurrences."

"Our imagination creates inner voices when we are beside ourselves," says the writer. "Spirits and inner voices are the delusions of the devil!"

But the text continues.

All release begins with movement, and Anette Svensson went up to the taxi-cab, took hold of the front bumper with both hands and without any real effort lifted up the whole vehicle; now released, the actor came to his senses immediately, got up and recited the lines from *The Tempest* that he had been so diligently searching for as he lay crushed under the cab: "If the devils came one at a time, I could fight my way through legions!"

The man with the drooping moustaches, the man in the midst of the absurdly over-fed women, now rushed up to Anette Svensson. She had calmly and carefully lowered the cab to the street again. He was panting, his voice was shrill but at the same time hoarse, while he talked to her he held her left upper arm in a bony but persuasive grip.

He explained that he was on the way to Toronto. The ladies in his company were the strongest in Sweden, the world championships in weight-lifting for ladies were going to be held in Toronto. He demanded that Anette Svensson should immediately join his troupe, indeed, he not only demanded: he implored her, he ordered her in the name of God and the National Swedish Athletics Association!

And yet once again she heard the inner voices: "Yes, Anette Svensson, nothing more will happen here, there everything can happen, never Here but There."

The competition was held in Borden Hall, Toronto.

Anette Svensson was weighed and put into the bantam-weight class.

The competitors had to lift a bar to whose end heavy metal discs had been attached. They were led to a stage one by one in front of an innumerable public that was muttering and grunting – thousands of people had come to Borden Hall. When the weighted bar had been lifted up into the air for a few fleeting seconds, the public roared with released passion which immediately subsided into a monotonous grumble of disappointment. No release lasts for ever.

The leader, he of the drooping moustache, Hemming by name – he had very hastily informed Anette Svensson that this was his name, it embarrassed him as it meant Loose Skin, he would much have preferred being called Powerful Body – this leader explained to Anette Svensson that she ought to make her first lift at the beginning of the contest.

"After that you can wait," he said; "when all the others are eliminated, then you go in and lift as many hundred kilos as necessary."

"A Mercedes!" he said. "A Mercedes with a driver! That weighs two tons."

All the competing ladies appeared uneasy and excited. They walked about with small tripping, bouncing resilient steps, they pulled and panted, they shook their vast limbs and cried Ahoo.

But Anette Svensson remained perfectly calm, yes indifferent. And of her indifference she thought: "It is the Spirit."

Then her turn came, her name and fatherland were called by a loudspeaker. Hemming offered her ammonia to sniff from a wad of cotton-wool and pushed her on to the stage. She smiled at the public; the stockinette dress that Hemming had lent her hung in heavy folds on her body; she had sprinkled her palms with talcum powder.

But she could not budge the weighted bar.

No, it lay immovable in spite of the fact that she tensed her sinews to bursting point and that she shouted Ahoo.

Only a hundred kilos and she could not even make it roll!

And within her she heard the Spirit: "One hundred kilos! Too little by half!"

"Yes of course," thought Anette Svensson. "What is a hundred kilos to the Spirit?"

The public muttered bitterly with disappointment. Anette Svensson resignedly made two more fruitless efforts to lift or at least to shift the weighted bar. Finally she bowed deeply three times and threw five kisses to the public. Through the thin cloth behind the stage she could hear Hemming weeping from disappointment and despair; she too could feel the tears tickling her throat and eyes, and, tottering uncertainly as if her frail body had lifted an unimaginable weight, she retreated backwards out of the glare of the footlights. The public did not even bother to whistle or mock her in any other way.

Hemming did not offer to comfort her with an embrace, no not even to offer her a red and white check handkerchief. He only groaned: "You are a disgrace to athletics!"

And she did not even manage to get her answer past her lips: "It's all the Spirit's fault!"

No, Anette Svensson crept away into a corner behind the toilets. There she sat while the contest proceeded and was decided, Ahoo, she sat motionless on a sand-box with her face pressed against her updrawn knees. She was a disgrace.

"Well, she has only herself to blame," says the writer. "She can very well do so. What the hell was she doing there with her inner voice and her Spirit?"

"Blame herself?" says the text, and raises its voice. "No person can ever blame himself. Don't imagine you can ever write a single line of which the meaning is 'blame yourself!' "

"Anette Svensson is not stupid," says the writer, "but she lacks intellectual discipline. For instance what did she do with her plastic basket with the sausage?"

"Not even you can blame yourself," says the text.

"Whatever you write you are blameless. And she forgot the plastic bag with the sausage and the carrots on the bus to Arlanda."

When the contests were over Hemming came up to her; the public and the ladies who had competed honestly were leaving Borden Hall; all of them were both satisfied and disappointed in different ways. Anette saw her image reflected in his eyes; a blot.

"You and your Mercedes," he said.

"With my own strength I can do nothing," she said. "I should have mentioned it to you. Everything depends on the Spirit that works in me."

"The Spirit?" he said.

"I don't know him very well," said Anette Svensson. "I have only quite recently had him. I got him at Åhlens on Klaraberg Street."

"I never buy anything at Åhlens," said Hemming, chewing his moustache angrily. "I bought a pair of leather gloves there once, and they were plastic. What sort of spirit is it you are talking about?"

"I don't know," said Anette Svensson.

"And what has he to do with weight-lifting?"

"The Spirit can lift anything whatever," said Anette Svensson. "That's all I know."

"But not a paltry hundred kilos?" said Hemming, without in any way trying to hide his scorn. He sneered at Anette Svensson and he sneered at the Spirit.

"Just so," said Anette Svensson. "A hundred kilos is too little by half for the Spirit."

"And what would be just right for it?" said Hemming. "Five hundred kilos? A couple of tons."

"You mustn't blaspheme," said Anette Svensson.

"I don't blaspheme," said Hemming. He had never before heard the word blaspheme.

"Four hundred kilos," said Anette Svensson. "The Spirit can't be bothered with lesser weights."

Then Hemming fetched a weighted bar and fastened new weights to its ends; they were now alone in the large room behind the stage. He pulled and groaned, but said not a word, he seemed to have quite forgotten the other ladies in his troupe – at last he fastened the discs with large screws. His movements were jerky and hasty, he was sweating with excitement and rage. At last he said: "Four hundred kilos! Now you can show what you and your Spirit are good for!"

"Four hundred kilos! That is more than any human being of whatever conceivable sex you please has ever lifted!"

And Anette Svensson took hold of the weighted bar with both her hands, lifted it, and held it with straight arms above her head. She had no need even to say Ahoo, it cost her no effort, she did not tremble, it seemed to her that the bar soared into the air by its own power.

If anyone doubts that this is true and that it really happened, the text will, in a decided, matter-of-fact voice, inform you that the name engraved on the polished steel bar was:

ELEIKO HALMSTAD SWEDEN

And Hemming looked at her. Tears filled his eyes, yes he really wept from emotion and happy impotence, he believed but his belief made him despair.

When she had again placed the bar on the floor he said: "Anette, you matchless talent, you must learn to lift like an ordinary woman. If you make an effort you will be able to lift a hundred kilos, with great difficulty a hundred and twenty kilos, if you force yourself to the uttermost you will lift a hundred and fifty."

And she said, "Hemming, you don't understand the situation properly."

"What you need is technical training," he said. "I will show you how an ordinary person lifts."

And with a quick movement he removed the six discs from the bar.

"Now!" he said. "Now you will see and learn. Now a new life will begin for you. Now you must watch my legs, my back, and my arms carefully."

He rapidly threw off his clothes; his underpants were adorned with the national coat of arms. And with an Ahoo that made his moustache flap like the wings of a bird he lifted the bar, he stamped his feet, the muscles of his arms and legs trembled and throbbed like anxious hearts under his skin, he lifted the bar on lightly bent arms and slightly crooked knees.

When he was about to bring his feet together and move his arms and legs something unexpected happened.

He seemed to be overcome by a moment of giddiness. His eyes squinted as if they were trying to turn inwards, he took two stumbling steps forwards, his hands and arms were twisted or bent backwards so that when he unavoidably fell forward he was hit by the bar that fell with him; it hit him an inch below his shoulder-blades, and there he lay.

Anette Svensson saw immediately that something serious had happened: blood was trickling from his nostrils, the bar was crushing his chest, now and then spasms shot through his outstretched hands, his chin and mouth, which were pressed against the floor, were twisted into an apathetic sneering grin. They were alone, the room was only lit by two weak ceiling lights; she looked for a telephone but could not find one. So she did what she had to do: with her left hand she lifted off the bar, she took him in her arms, he weighed little, and she carried him out through a door to the left of the stage EMERGENCY EXIT, down a narrow spiral staircase, along a long corridor – he was as limp as a rag doll and his skin was sticky with sweat – out through a heavy iron door and into the street.

"If only he had not been so horribly strong and so frightfully weak it would never have happened," she thought and tears collected and made a milk-white pool on his chest. A taxi-cab stopped and its driver looked long and thoughtfully at Anette Svensson and Hemming, a weeping woman holding a limp naked man in her arms. He recognized it, it was a picture he had seen in his childhood, an old painting or a sculpture, the sight gripped him in a strange way and he drove them to the Hospital of the Virgin Mary.

"Was this absolutely necessary?" asks the writer.

"Yes," answers the text. "Necessary and obvious and unavoidable."

Hemming recovered consciousness after forty-eight hours. She kept watch by his bed. Or more correctly: a third part of himself recovered consciousness. His back was broken, the whole of his splendid body below his fifth rib was sadly useless.

And he said to her: "It's all your fault."

To this naturally enough she had no answer.

For three weeks he remained at the Hospital of the Virgin Mary. After that he was transported home. The Swedish Society of Weight-lifters paid the expenses. Anette Svensson went with him – it was all her fault.

Out over the Atlantic, that terrifying void between sky and sea, he asked her, and he shouted out his question for his stretcher was placed in the tail of the plane close to the engine: "You'll never leave me will you?"

She didn't want to answer, but all the same there was a piercing, heart-rending answer from within her: "Only death can part us!"

Hemming had previously never had a woman, he had only had the gigantic ladies. Now Anette Svensson moved in with him in his little flat in Piper's Street. She became his nurse, she trimmed his moustache and boiled his six eggs every morning, she emptied his urine bag when it was full and she washed his wasting body; it was wasting away in spite of all the eggs he ate and in spite of the fact that he believed his bone-marrow would grow together again, and every evening she read aloud to him from the evening paper's sports pages and some bits out of the *Guinness Book of Records*.

Yes, you could almost say that her hands carried him through life, Ahoo. They were not married, there was no reason for them to be married, she was his woman and he was her invalid, they were united by a bond that was infinitely stronger than any marriage could ever have been: her ineffaceable debt to him. Hemming always called Anette his wife.

Seven years passed and they never asked from whence she got the strength she needed for this ceaseless lifting and carrying, this many-sided heaving and lugging, this awe-inspiring weight-lifting. But both were convinced that the strength was called the Spirit, and in their heart of hearts they carried the conviction that the Spirit should be called the Holy.

Sometimes she said to him: "I love you." That too she owed him, it had to be borne. And sometimes he would grasp her hands without any obvious reason, and hold them fast, and only scrutinize them. He wanted to see the Spirit.

And he suggested that they should go on tour, and that for money she should display her strength, and he reckoned up for her all the things she could lift: blocks of concrete, buses, men piled one on top of the other, drums of oil, ponies. But she said: "You are enough for me."

146

"I take it we are nearing the end?" says the writer.

"Don't ask me," says the text. "In this instance the lifting and carrying and lugging can go on for an eternity."

"I don't trust you," says the writer. "Above all I don't trust that thing called the Spirit."

"On the contrary!" answers the text. "I truly wish that I was less predictable and that the Spirit was more unpredictable!"

"First you decide the rules of the game!" says the writer. "And then you complain that you must follow them!"

"I would willingly stop here," says the text. Here in the warmth and tenderness of Piper's Street 29, 3rd floor. Anette Svensson was in the habit of carrying him downstairs and up, he constantly wanted to go on trips, to athletic contests, to remarkable sights which in his immobility he was afraid of forgetting, to inns where, in the days of his strength, he had eaten unforgettable portions. But a text may never think of its own convenience, it must drain itself to the bottom, and only show its true face at the end.

"I chose between weight-lifting and rock-climbing," Hemming was in the habit of saying. "We have no Alps, so it turned out to be weight-lifting." And Anette Svensson who had chosen neither weight-lifting nor rock-climbing felt that she was more and more often occupied with both. She lifted and carried the weight of the Spirit, of Hemming and of her fault up the hill of Meaninglessness.

If she had ever grown tired she would have greeted weariness as recreation and a let-up. The ease with which she carried even the heaviest burden bored her to death.

She was now twenty-eight. And she saw before her the long length of the life that remained, thirty, forty, fifty years of this horrible strength.

How does one free oneself of strength, how does one acquire weakness?

At last she knew, she heard it said within herself: by a repulsive exercise of strength, with a lift so horrible that it could never be repeated, she would be able to secure by force the weakness she needed.

It was a Sunday in May, he wanted to see Stockholm once more from the Katarina lift. She carried him downstairs to the car, drove to Slussen, lifted him over to his wheelchair, took the lift up to the bridge. It was a sunny but cool day with no wind.

She looked at Hemming and the wheelchair and Stockholm.

"Stockholm weighs seventeen billion tons," said Hemming.

"Yes," said Anette Svensson, "there are weights that are completely inhuman."

"All the same everything is held on high," said Hemming.

"Yes," she said. "It is odd."

"As soon as there is anything that needs carrying, a suitable strength is sure to crop up," said Hemming.

"Yes," she said. "There are no doubt enormously many more strengths than we can ever imagine."

"Continents, towns, and people," he said. "Everything is carried. It is no doubt some sort of a law of nature."

She looked at him intently, lately his shoulders had begun to slouch forwards, and he smiled all the time.

"At the time I could hold myself up by my own strength I never felt as safe as I do now."

Yes, there sat Hemming and positively shone with trustfulness.

And now Anette Svensson heard something within her pointing out that the time had arrived. She lifted him gently from his wheelchair – he lay warm and thankful against her – she lifted him in outstretched arms above her head, why, he even giggled with titillated delight, and she threw him in a wide arc over the safety railing. She was full of the chill of the Spirit and had no need to exert herself. Later she said to the prosecutor: "Hemming threw himself."

Ahoo.

And while he was falling, while rotating, limp but at the same time struggling he plunged downwards, he cried: "It is not the Holy Spirit! It is not the Holy Spirit!"

But none of the onlookers, the few who happened to be present, took any notice of his cries. They didn't take him seriously. They all saw how clumsy and ugly and deformed his body was, and no one could understand why he was yelling that his was not the Holy Spirit. Everyone knows that the Holy Spirit is a dove who sinks down slowly.

"Have you now said what you want to say about that thing, the Spirit?" asks the writer.

"One can never say what one wants to," says the text.

"And Anette Svensson? Why did you lay her open to this devilish illusion?"

"In order to purify her of her innocent lack of a view of life. To bring her to an awareness of it."

"Awareness of it?"

"Yes. I must have some excuse," says the text.

"Of what should she become aware?"

"I don't know. She doesn't even know herself yet, she only sits still in a cell, and a wardress has to feed her, since she cannot think of lifting anything, not even her hands."

"And the Spirit?"

"That," says the text. "Oh, I have put that back in one of the freezer compartments in Åhlens at Klaraberg Street, the one with fish and shellfish, between the cod and the crab. It was there I got it."

# James, the Poor in Spirit

This is how it was: God created the world by speaking with thirty-two voices. He divided the world into three books, one for the sea, one for the earth, and one for the air, and He collected the three books into one volume which He called the universe. When He spoke with the thirty-two voices He used twenty-two letters: the three letters that were the mothers of all the other letters, alath, mem, and shin and in addition seven double letters and twelve single. And about the world He set a boundary that was the number ten: Ten that within itself bore the five eternally opposite pairs, the ten Incompatibles which incessantly strove against each other and by their strife maintained the eternal movement that is called life, these ten totally different things that He united into five indissoluble marriages; east and west, north and south, evil and goodness, height and depth, beginning and end. And He Himself lived in the whole that He had created, as fire lives in coal.

This is the simple way in which existence appeared to James the son of Alphaeus.

In order to conform with creation in a respectable and exemplary manner he had himself married Mariam, daughter of Hurais.

He had paid ten shekels of silver for her, a cheap price. As a bridal gift he had given her ten ells of red linen, a veil and an enormous spray of myrtle. She hung the spray of myrtle by the door, sewed herself a cloak of the linen and bore him three sons in the space of three years.

But after that he chanced to become one of the twelve disciples.

Jesus of Nazareth preached that God would soon dissolve His laws, nothing would remain, not the twenty-two letters, nor the sea, the earth and the heavens, nor the five pairs of opposites, He would create everything anew. And James wanted to be part of it right from the beginning so that he might with certainty experience the end.

He therefore left Mariam and his three sons in Capernaum, he even left his humble occupation with the town's customs office, he left everything in spite of the fact that Mariam wept and questioned him: "James, should not our union last for ever?"

And James answered: "He shall dissolve everything."

So he joined Peter, Andrew and the other nine disciples, the Master led and they followed Him.

But Mariam, she who was left behind, first felt peculiar distress; she was filled by a corroding compassion for herself; for two days and two nights she lay unconscious and her three sons sat whimpering beside her bed, but then she got up, she decided to endure, to submit herself to being abandoned.

She carried out into the yard all the little things that had belonged to him and burned them: the tattered sandals, the broken comb he had used for his beard, the spoon of goat's horn, the little reed flute, the three-legged post on which his cloak had hung, the fly-swatter of plaited grasses, his puttees that he had never used.

When that was done she began to weep again, she wept so much that she went blind for a month; a black animal seemed to be devouring her from within.

And she was struck by dumbness, so that she could not say anything to her three sons, but was obliged to whip and beat them to make them understand her.

The women of Capernaum came to tell her everything that was being said about James; about how he was wandering about the country with the band of disciples, now he was here now he was there, how he was associating with thieves and prostitutes and vagabonds. "Don't grieve for him," they said, "be thankful that you were rid of him at last."

"About whom are you talking?" said Mariam. "James? I had forgotten him."

But the truth was that she longed for him so that she spat blood, and her belly swelled up and became like a faulty wine skin. Her breasts were filled with tiny cracks and a pale milk-like liquid oozed from them.

And she had to take down the spray of myrtle once a week from its hook and carry it carefully outside to let the wind blow it free of dust.

After two years had passed these torments were over: James's Master had been executed in Jerusalem, but in spite of this he had not returned home, and she realized that he had not only cast her off, he had forgotten her, and those parts of her body that had previously swelled and overflowed with longing now began to shrink and shrivel with resignation.

As she grew increasingly thin and bony she brought up her three sons. What she needed for the necessities of life she got from her father-in-law Alphaeus, who was deeply ashamed of his wastrel son. She brought up her sons to be timorous, indeed anguished and in all they did dutiful young men. She succeeded in obtaining places in the Customs Department for two of them; the third became part-owner of a fishing-boat in Magdala.

In the matter of God's recreation of the world James became more and more uncertain. Perhaps He had already made every-thing anew, but in a way that James had not succeeded in discovering. Perhaps it was going to happen in the time to come, in which case it was just a matter of patiently awaiting these coming times. One by one the disciples broke up from Jerusalem – those who had not been killed during the first difficult years. They were to carry his Message to all the four cardinal points, preferably to the four corners of the earth, provided that cardinal points and corners still existed. James was to found a community in Gamala, after that he was to proceed eastwards.

He had really completely forgotten Mariam and his three sons.

And he only remembered the Message uncertainly and incompletely.

His preaching was filled with words like perhaps, it may be, possibly, probably and it may be thought that . . .

In the end it seemed to him as if just uncertainty and the honest account of irresolution were the Message itself. He never preached about God's thirty-two voices, the three books, the twenty-two letters, the five pairs of opposites, no, not even once about the Law; perhaps all had been got rid of and destroyed, perhaps not.

He was poor in spirit, that was all he knew. That knowledge made him exceedingly humble. And that humility made him devout, yes, he was the most devout man in Gamala.

Unfortunately his preaching did not win him any devoted followers. But he got a number of friends. His friends became his congregation, they congregated round his devoutness.

And he never got farther than to Gamala. There in confidence and doubt he awaited the final remoulding of existence.

His back became bent, his hair and beard turned white, he stopped eating, he had no need of other nourishment than humility and devoutness. He ceased to speak, he delivered the Message with his eyes and with the careful movement of his hands, he had forgotten the name of the devil and he finally died a virgin.

On the morning that Mariam got to hear that he was dead and was lying in state in Gamala she took down the spray of myrtle from its place by the door – it was now stained with mildew – she dressed herself in the red linen cloak, on her feet she bound her toughest sandals, and then she set off. She walked with great strength and determination, bending forwards with long strides, her knees bent. She swung the spray of myrtle in her right hand, now and then she used it as a stick to help her to walk faster – she was afraid they would have time to bury him – her red cloak flapped in the wind from the Lake of Gennesar.

By evening she had arrived. She stood by his bier.

His hands were clasped over his breast, his aged head gleamed with peace; she could clearly see that he had undoubtedly forgotten her long ago.

She gazed at him; his friends, those he was in the habit of calling his congregation, drew back timorously when they felt the fearful chill that emanated from her, they retreated and left her alone with him, wife with husband.

Her face, that face which had once been gentle and bright, so gentle and so bright that, before he became an apostle, James had not been able to withstand it, that face was now dark and harsh. Mortification and bitterness, which had been her only distraction for many years, had scratched it and lined it and covered it with dark streaks.

When they had been left alone she moved up to the head of the bier, she bent over him and recited three times with a strange tenderness in her voice a curse over the man who, because of falseness and faithlessness, would never be granted one day of rest or satisfaction or refreshment in the realm of death. Then she spat in his face seven times, seven good mouthfuls of sticky saliva and expectoration. Finally she lifted up the spray of myrtle, that withered bone-dry spray of myrtle and rammed it with all the strength she had into his right eye, rammed it so hard that it was not halted until it reached the bone at the back of his neck.

And James felt that the final upheaval had at last taken place. To him it seemed that everything was suddenly made anew, that unimaginable wealth and heavenly joy had come to him, understanding that would endure for eternity. He felt as if he were a coal in whose innermost being fire dwelt.

To have had something to abandon, something that even in your very bones you can blot out by abandoning! To have owned someone whose love showed itself to be as inextinguishable as the deepest hatred! To have been the object of a love which even in death refused to let itself be rejected.

And he sat up, he rose from the death-bed on which he lay. He dried the horrid curse and the sticky spittle from his face, the dry mildewy spray of myrtle still stuck out of his eye, he stood up and faced her, took her in his arms and made love to her on the spot.